A HOME WITH

Men of the Border Lands 2

Marla Monroe

MENAGE EVERLASTING

Siren Publishing, Inc.
www.SirenPublishing.com

A SIREN PUBLISHING BOOK
IMPRINT: Ménage Everlasting

A HOME WITH THEM
Copyright © 2011 by Marla Monroe

ISBN-10: 1-61926-403-X
ISBN-13: 978-1-61926-403-8

First Printing: December 2011

Cover design by Les Byerley
All art and logo copyright © 2011 by Siren Publishing, Inc.

Printed in the U.S.A.

PUBLISHER
Siren Publishing, Inc.
www.SirenPublishing.com

A HOME WITH THEM

Men of the Border Lands 2

MARLA MONROE
Copyright © 2011

Chapter One

Jessie cowered in the bathtub, squeezing as far back behind the shower curtain as she could get. She hadn't shut the door, in hopes they wouldn't think she was in there. She also left the shower curtain partially open, so they wouldn't think to look further. It had worked in the past when they came looking for her. She hoped it would work again. She didn't want to think of the consequences if they caught her.

She could hear the men rambling around, knocking things over, and tearing through the closet next to the bathroom. This was the second time they had come looking for her. Ever since the year of catastrophes, the world was in a mess. Governments had fallen after massive tornadoes, hurricanes, earthquakes, and tsunamis had devastated the lands. Then came the plagues that left less than a third of the population in the United States alive.

Now it was called New America, and people fought each other for everything, most especially for females. There were very few left in the world, and a lot of major fights were centered around who possessed a female.

God, where are Wyatt and Kent? They're going to find me this time. I just know it.

Jessie was sure her heart was beating loud enough they could hear it if they stopped making so much noise, and if not her heart, then her breathing. She couldn't stop panting. It felt like an elephant was sitting on her chest, and she couldn't draw in a full breath.

"She's here. There has to be some secret room or something somewhere," one of the men said.

How many were there? She had no idea, but at least two. If the men didn't get back soon, she was going to be found. They rarely left her alone without at least one of them staying with her, but they had to work so they would have enough to eat in the next few days. They helped clear out buildings that were still standing but full of debris. In exchange, they received food coupons.

There was more stomping around in the other part of the little house they were living in. Then someone returned to the bathroom and jerked back the shower curtain. She screamed and tried to fight him. He yelled in triumph, then harrumphed in pain when her knee made contact with his groin.

"Bitch!" He grabbed her around the throat and dragged her out of the tub. "I got her, Joe."

The other man ran into the bedroom with a nasty-looking grin on his face. "She's a beaut, Sam. She'll get us a good price."

"I'm giving her a ride first," Sam said.

Jessie couldn't scream or do much of anything with his hand around her neck and Joe holding her arms. Where were Wyatt and Kent? She really needed them to come home now.

"Come on, we can fuck her once we get her home. Them boys will be back soon enough," Joe said.

Sam let go of her throat and helped Joe tie her arms behind her back. Then he threw her over his shoulder and they headed toward the front of the house and the door. Try as she may, she couldn't scream. All that would come out was a hoarse shout. Not that anyone would get involved when it came to a female, unless they wanted to fight for her.

Just as they reached the front door where they'd kicked it in, Wyatt and Kent walked up. Wyatt gave an enraged roar and attacked the second man while Kent went after Sam. The man dropped her hard on the floor and tried to defend himself, but Kent was much bigger and in better shape. They kicked the two men's asses, but couldn't kill them. Murder was punishable by death in New America. No jury or judge, just a swift bullet through the brain.

They picked the two men up and threw them in the back of their truck.

"We catch you around here again and I just might make you disappear. No body means no death penalty," Wyatt said with a growl in his voice.

Kent hurried over to where Jessie lay and untied her. He took one look at her throat and pulled her into his arms.

"Fuck, Wyatt, they choked her. She's got handprints around her neck." He picked her up and carried her back into the house and gently laid her on the couch.

"We can't keep doing this, Kent. One day they, or someone else, are going to get her. We've got to go west. They say there's land out there you can make a living off of. At least there aren't as many people out there to protect her from."

Jessie tried to speak, but her voice was so hoarse she gave up. Instead, she laid her head against Kent's chest, wrapped in his arms. She knew she was a burden to them and wondered why they cared. They had always treated her like a kid sister. They'd grown up on the same street back in Kentucky. Now they lived in the next town. Theirs had been totally destroyed by a tornado and then a flood. She sighed and hoped they could figure something out. She didn't think her luck would hold much longer.

* * * *

Kent sat at the opposite end of the couch and pulled Jessie's feet in his lap. He shook his head at the condition of the front door. It would be impossible to repair it this time. They'd need a new door, and that cost credits. Wyatt was right. They had to do something else. Living here wasn't working.

"Who do we know that has been out west? We need to have some idea of what we're doing before we take off."

Wyatt nodded his head. "David Langston has been out west. I don't know how far, but we can talk to him."

"Then let's go talk to him. He'll understand what we have to do. He lost his daughter to the black market."

"Now is as good a time as any. Come on. Jessie is going with us. I'm not letting her out of our sight from now on." Wyatt eased from behind Jessie then helped her stand up.

"Feel like a short walk, Jessie?"

"Yes," she whispered in a hoarse voice.

Kent gritted his teeth at her obvious pain. They had nothing to give her for it, either. He led the way through the splintered front door and down the street to where David lived. He still had his original house and shared it with two young teens he had taken under his wing.

He knocked at the door and waited for someone to answer the door. They could hear footsteps coming down the hall. David himself opened the door after checking through the window.

"Kent, Jessie, Wyatt. Come on in. What can I do for you?" He led them into the living room and offered them a seat.

"We need some information about the west lands," Kent said.

"They're called the Border Lands once you get past the Kansas area," the other man said. "Why do you want to know about them?"

"We need to know what to expect, and the best way to get there. We can't stay here anymore. They almost got Jessie today. They hurt her. Look at her throat." Wyatt pulled her hair back from her neck so David could see.

"Aw, hell, man." He let out a deep breath and nodded. "I guess you're right. I don't like it, but you don't really have much of a choice. I'd go with you and show you the way, but I can't leave the boys here, and I'm not getting any younger."

"We wouldn't expect you to. We just need all the information you can give us." Kent hoped they were making the right decision.

"You're going to need to take everything of worth that you can with you to barter for food along the way. They don't use food coupons out there. You can raid some of the towns on the way for canned goods if there are any left. Just be aware that wild animals, especially wolves, have taken up residence in the bigger cities. They make dens in the open buildings."

David sat with them for over two hours telling them what to expect. Then he got out a map and drew the course they needed to take to avoid some areas and pass through some of the safer towns where people still lived.

"Once you get deeper into the Border Lands, you can squat at a homestead where no one is living and take up residence. You will need to clean the place up quick and start a garden as soon as you arrive so you'll have food for the winter. Gather up any cattle and chickens you can get hold of. You can also get wild game out of the woods out there. I don't know what more I can tell you." David handed Kent the folded map.

"You've told us more than enough. We'll start packing up early tomorrow and head out. Anyplace has to be better than here," Wyatt said.

"Just remember you're going to be living real primitive out there. You will likely not have electricity and have to use a well for water."

"We'll prepare ourselves." Kent stood up and shook David's hand.

"You take good care of your woman there, boys. She's precious and worth anything it takes to keep her safe."

"We know. We plan to take good care of her." Wyatt shook his hand and ushered them back to the front door.

They heard the locks turn behind them once they were outside. It was just before getting dark.

"We need to hurry home and board up the door as best as we can." Wyatt led with Jessie between them.

Kent went over everything in his head, making plans for what they needed to pack up and how they were going to fit it all in their truck. It would be a tough fit. Maybe they could add to it once they found a city to scavenge.

He was worried about the primitive aspect of the Border Lands. They were used to living with electricity and running water. Even though a lot of places did without, they still had it there. They also had fresh food from the supply trucks that came through. They weren't used to roughing it.

He got a great idea. They could use a U-Haul truck. There were several outside of town at an old service station. Surely they could trade their truck for one if there was anyone even claiming them. It was a fairly new truck in great condition with very few miles on it. They saved gas by walking almost everywhere they went.

He waited until they were safely inside with the door nailed shut and the couch in front of it before relaying his thoughts to the others.

"That's a good idea. We can fit a lot of stuff in one and add whatever we scavenge along the way." Wyatt placed a kiss on Jessie's forehead and urged her to go lie down for a while.

"I'm going to take the truck and see if I can swap it tonight. We need to get packed up in the morning and get on the road," Kent said.

"You be careful. It's not safe out there, at night especially."

"I will be. I should be back within the hour."

Kent went out the back door and circled around to the truck. He cranked it and pulled out of the drive, heading to the service station and the U-Hauls. It took all of ten minutes to get across town. When he pulled into the service station, no one came out to greet him. In fact, the place looked in bad shape. He climbed out of his truck and walked around, looking for a sign that anyone took care of the place.

The windows were all broken, and there didn't appear to be anything much left worth taking in the place. He combed the inside for keys and found a box with them jumbled up in it. He took the entire box out to the parking lot where the trucks were parked. It took a good twenty minutes before he found a key that fit the largest of the trucks. It cranked right up. He checked the gas gauge and found it was half-full. He pulled up to the pump and attempted to turn the electricity on. It flickered inside, but the pumps turned on. He filled the tank, then grabbed one of the trailers and hooked it to the back.

After turning off the electricity again, he emptied everything from his truck into the U-Haul and scavenged everything from the other trucks he could find. Then he climbed back into the truck and drove toward home and his family.

Wyatt was watching for him when he drove up in the front of the house. He backed the truck up to the front door and locked the truck before circling around back to go in the back door.

"Have any trouble?"

"Not a soul around. I think we need to grab a couple of hours sleep, then pack up and leave before dawn," Kent said.

"I agree. People see us loading up and they're liable to try and take everything from us." Wyatt looked around at the house. "There really isn't that much we need to load. There will be a few pieces of furniture. I think we need to take the mattresses so we have somewhere to sleep on the way."

"What are we going to do about Jessie, Wyatt?"

"What do you mean?"

"She's old enough to know we want her. It's been hell all these years living with her and not being with her." Kent ran a hand over his head.

"Hell, I don't know. She's made overtures and pranced around half-naked often enough. I'm just not sure she's ready for both of us."

"I vote we see how things progress as we travel. One thing is for sure. If we are questioned, she's our woman. We've got to be sure she knows that as well."

Wyatt nodded and followed Kent upstairs to the bedrooms. They slept on either side of Jessie's room. Kent had wanted her since the day she turned sixteen. That had been over five years ago, just after things had begun to settle down from the plagues. She had been left without any family, and he and Wyatt had stepped in and taken her with them. She hadn't questioned and didn't seem to regret it at all.

Wyatt wanted her just as much as Kent did, but he was older and felt more responsible for her. He didn't want to take advantage of her because they were her guardians, so to speak. Kent wasn't sure that he felt like a guardian to her. All he knew was that she was beautiful.

Jessie's long brown hair was the color of a mink coat and softer than rabbit's fur. It almost reached to her waist. She normally kept it pulled back and braided it, making her look much younger than her twenty-one years. She had eyes the color of honey and a smile that took his heart. She had a woman's body with curves in all the right places. He and his brother were both six feet six inches, and she fit perfectly under their chins. She was perfect for them. He just had to get Wyatt to see it.

He didn't see anything wrong with sharing her. Maybe back before the catastrophes when there were plenty of women it would have been wrong, but now, he saw more and more men sharing their women. Of course, a lot of them had bought them on the black market. He didn't agree with that one bit. Women weren't commodities to be bought and sold. It was what they were fighting to keep Jessie safe from.

Finally, his mind stilled, and Kent was able to settle down and catch some sleep. They had a long day tomorrow. It would be the first of many long days, he was sure.

Chapter Two

Wyatt woke up about three the next morning and groaned. He really needed another two hours of sleep, but they needed to get a move on. He snuck down the hall past Jessie's room to wake Kent up. His brother was instantly awake when Wyatt opened the door.

"Time to get a move on." Wyatt backed out so his brother could dress.

He didn't plan on waking Jessie up until they had to, or she woke up first. She needed to rest as much as possible. This was going to be harder on her than any of them. She would have to stick with them and not have any freedoms at all. Not that she had a lot here.

"What's first?" Kent asked.

"Let's open the front up and move any furniture we plan to take, then box up the clothes from our rooms and the food out of the kitchen. We'll save the mattress for last so we can sleep in the back of the truck at night. Since Jessie has the king bed, we'll use her mattress. We can't afford to take all of them. We need the room for storing whatever we come across that we might need."

Kent nodded and started moving the couch out of the way of the door. They worked for a solid two hours before Jessie came downstairs in sleeping shorts to see what they were doing.

"Man, you've moved a lot of stuff already. Why didn't you wake me up to help?"

"Because you needed your rest. You're still hoarse from last night," Wyatt pointed out.

She blanched, and he cursed himself for reminding her of her ordeal.

"Come here, honey." He wrapped her in his arms and almost groaned out loud at the feel of her breasts against his chest. God, yes, he wanted her.

"What can I do now that I'm up?"

"Get dressed and pack up all your clothes and bathroom stuff."

He watched her run up the stairs and disappear around the landing. It was hard to believe he was only four years older than her. At twenty-four, he felt like an old man. He guessed having so much responsibility made him feel older. Kent was twenty-two and had had a crush on Jessie ever since she'd been a teenager. He'd discouraged it until now. Now he knew she was old enough, and things had changed in their lives. They would have to become a family to survive in the world now.

"Did I hear Jessie?" Kent asked.

"Yeah, I sent her up to pack her things. How much more do we have in the kitchen?"

"I've gotten all the canned stuff and the appliances. Do you want to take any of the frozen stuff to eat as it slowly thaws?"

"Fill a cooler with it, and we'll see how it works. We can always cook over a fire. Which reminds me, we need to take the racks out of the oven with us to use for a campfire."

"Good idea."

They worked in silence, packing up their lives and everything around them. Jessie brought down a load of her things, and Kent took it from her to add to the truck. He followed her upstairs to help her with the rest while Wyatt arranged things in the truck. He checked his watch. It was closing in on six. They needed to get moving.

"How much more is there?" he asked Kent when he brought in a box.

"Not much. She packed our bathrooms up, too, so we don't have that to finish."

"Good girl." He pulled her into a hug when she set her box down. "Let's get a move on so we can get on the road.

"What about breakfast?" Jessie asked.

"I kept the cereal boxes out for us to munch on for now. We'll see after that. There's a six-pack of water in the front of the cab as well, so we'll be okay."

Jessie nodded, and for the first time, he saw real fear on her face. It wasn't the same fear from the men who'd tried to kidnap her. It was the fear of the unknown. He knew exactly how she felt, but he couldn't let on to her. He had to project confidence for her and Kent.

They loaded up the last box and closed the doors to the van. Wyatt latched the door, then added a padlock. He made sure Kent had a key as well in case something happened to him. They climbed up into the cab of the big U-Haul and pulled out with the trailer behind them. They had a lot of strange looks as they headed through town toward the highway, but no one tried to stop them.

Wyatt began to feel a little easier as they left the town of Holly Bluff behind them. They had a hell of a journey ahead of them, but with a little help from the good Lord, they would make it. David had marked on the map everywhere he thought there was gas along the way, so they stopped and filled up even if all they needed was a fourth of a tank. They didn't want to end up stranded with no way to get gas.

Oddly enough, the first two places they stopped took old money as trade. They stocked up at the little station on water and canned goods, as well as snack food. They traded a thawing chicken for supper that first night in a little community about nine hours out of Holly Bluff. The woman who took it offered them a homemade meal of fried fish and potatoes along with the use of her driveway for them to bed down in the truck. Her husband hadn't been too keen on it but shut up at the prospect of chicken for supper the next night.

Their first night was awkward. They put Jessie between them on the mattress in the back of the truck and slept on either side of her. She didn't seem to worry about it and was almost instantly asleep. He and Kent lay awake for long minutes, trying to control their libidos and calm down after the long day of driving.

"Wyatt? Think we'll get there in four days?"

"Don't know, Kent. Will depend on how accurate David's map is. He said he hadn't gone that far, and we'll probably want to go farther than he did. I think we're looking at maybe five days."

"Going to be a long five nights," Kent said.

"Yeah, you could say that. Go to sleep. We've got to get going in the morning. I don't trust that husband of hers. He wasn't happy about us being here. I wouldn't be surprised if he didn't call a friend or two to check out our things."

"Fuck, are we ever going to be able to trust anyone again?"

"I don't know, maybe. We don't know how the Border Lands will be. Maybe things will be better there. Now get some rest."

* * * *

Jessie woke before the guys did and stretched. She hadn't slept that well in a long time. She was sure it was because she'd slept between the only two people in the world she truly trusted. It helped that she loved them, too. She'd been in love with them for the last two years. Before that, she'd had crushes on them, but somewhere along the way, she fell hard for them.

Early on she'd felt confused over feeling the same feelings for both of them. Then she figured out that they weren't the exact same feelings. She loved different things about each of them.

Wyatt was the oldest, with shaggy black hair that reached his shoulders when he didn't cut it. When he did, it curled at his ears. Right now, it was long again. He had the darkest eyes she'd ever seen. They were so black she could see herself in them. He had a dry sense of humor and tended to reprimand her when she got out of line.

Kent, on the other hand, was more laid back and often got in the middle of her and Wyatt when they knocked heads over something. He was equally handsome, with black hair that was straight and cut close to his head. He actually did it himself with an electric trimmer.

He'd often threatened to cut Wyatt's hair with it on several occasions. His eyes were a rich hazel, with more brown flecks than green. They seemed to change colors with his moods.

Both men were broad shouldered, with tapered waists and delightfully rounded asses. They had strong legs the size of tree limbs, and since she'd been living with them for five years, she'd had reason to see them in every stage of dress and undress, so she knew all about their cocks. She dreamed about their cocks. They each sported a hefty package between their legs that would rival a porn star.

Sadly, though, they didn't seem to see her as a woman. They were still stuck in her teenage days, and it drove her crazy. She wanted them to notice her as a woman, one with needs that only they could fill. One day, though. She would get through to them that she wasn't some shrinking violet that wouldn't know what to do with them if they came on to her. She knew what she'd do. She'd jump their bones.

"Kent? Can you hear me?" She touched his shoulder. He immediately rolled over and grabbed her. She screeched.

"Hell, Jessie. Don't scare me like that."

"Scare you? All I did was call your name."

Wyatt yawned and turned irritated eyes toward them.

"What is going on?"

"Don't we need to get up and get on the road?" Jessie asked them.

Wyatt looked at his watch and cursed. It was late. He scrambled out of the covers and started pulling on clothes. Kent did the same thing. Jessie watched them with lust in her thoughts, then grabbed her things and walked to the front of the truck where there was a separation of sorts made up of furniture. She changed out of her sleeping clothes into jeans and a T-shirt. She grabbed a jacket and shrugged into it because it was a bit cold this time of morning. Spring hadn't quite sprung yet.

When she came back out, the men were dressed and shoving the mattress back toward the other furniture.

"Let's get up front, Jessie," Kent said, taking her hand.

Wyatt jumped down from the back and held up his arms to help Jessie down. She loved how strong he was. It felt good to be held by him. Kent jumped down from the truck, and they closed and locked the latch into place. Wyatt checked to make sure the trailer was still properly hooked up and climbed up in the cab of the truck beside them.

"Okay, let's get on the road again. We'll stop at the next place and see about breakfast." Wyatt pulled back out onto the highway.

Jessie had never seen anything like it. There were abandoned cars all along the road. At least the road was clear in most areas. Sometimes they had to drive around a car or truck, which always made her nervous. She kept expecting to see skeletons in them and didn't want to freak out around the men. They already thought of her as a helpless girl.

They drove through several small towns that looked deserted, but Wyatt didn't want to stop at any of them since they weren't marked on the map by David as safe places. Finally, around ten that morning, they pulled into a city that was marked on the map as basically deserted. This was one of the places that David suggested they do some scavenging.

Wyatt drove through the streets, often having to drive up on sidewalks to get around vehicles in the roads. He found a small grocery store and pulled in close to the doors. They looked all around but didn't see any wolves or other animals anywhere.

"Jessie, stay in the truck with the doors locked while we check it out. If there's any trouble, honk the horn." Wyatt looked over at Kent and nodded.

She watched them climb out of the truck and lock the doors behind them. They slowly walked toward the doors and pushed at the door. It actually opened. They looked back at her and kept on going until they disappeared inside the building. She waited and waited for what seemed like hours before Kent walked out and signaled that she could some in. As she climbed out of the truck, he reminded her to walk slowly and not run.

"There could be wolves watching us. Just walk slowly."

"Is there anything much left?" she asked when she reached Kent.

"Yeah, quite a bit of good stuff. Here's a cart. Go up and down the aisles and grab whatever you think we need that isn't out-of-date. We're starting on the opposite side. Make sure there aren't any bugs crawling around on it or around it."

"Ew, gross."

He laughed and left her with her cart to search his assigned area. Jessie took the cart and began scanning the contents of the aisle she was in. She grabbed all the canned foods she could reach, paying close attention to expiration dates. The meats were closer to expired than the vegetables. She even found some non-expired tuna fish. She moved on to the next row and felt like she'd hit the jackpot. It was the canned fruit row. She loaded up on everything that appeared to still be good.

Kent wheeled his full cart over to her and took a look. He smiled and pointed to his bounty.

"I'm going to load this up and be back to grab yours next. Fill it up, girl."

Jessie redoubled her efforts to have a full cart by the time he got back to her. When he did, he traded her full cart with his empty one. With what could only be called a mischievous expression, Kent leaned in and kissed her. She opened to him without thought and welcomed his tongue with hers. They teased each other for a few seconds, then Kent pulled away with a sigh. Jessie licked her lips, enjoying the taste of him.

A few minutes later, Wyatt walked up with a cart full of water.

"How are you all doing?" he asked.

"Fine. I've emptied my buggy, and I'm about to go empty hers. She's got two more rows to go down, and then we'll be finished here."

"Hurry it up, baby. We need to check out a sporting goods store for supplies."

Jessie all but ran up and down the aisles, grabbing things as she went. When she got to the pharmacy area, she grabbed every pain reliever they had and all of the cold and cough remedies. Then she grabbed all the first aid supplies she had room for on the cart. She even stuffed things under the buggy. When she wheeled it over to the front of the store, Wyatt's eyes got big and he grinned.

"You are a typical woman. You like to shop."

She punched him in the arm and helped him unload it into containers and milk crates from the back of the store to carry outside. By the time they had finished, she was exhausted. She realized she was going to have to toughen up to make it in their new world. She didn't want to be a burden on them.

They stopped at a sporting goods store next and loaded up on all the guns and ammunition they could find. It was obvious that someone else had been through things there. Jessie grabbed coats and boots in all their sizes, as well as camping gear. They finished off with a few fishing items and decided that was plenty.

"Let's grab some gas and then get back on the road. We've got another three or four hours of sun left," Wyatt said.

Jessie climbed back in the cab of the truck and scooted over to sit up against Wyatt while she waited on Kent to climb in behind her. Wyatt pushed her over and gave her a strange look. She didn't let it faze her. She was going to figure out a way to get them to see her as a woman one way or another.

"Okay, last stop, gas and maybe snacks if they have anything that's not out-of-date." Wyatt started the big truck and drove to what looked to be an old truck stop.

Inside, nothing was left other than a few dry goods. The good thing was that the place still had electricity, so they were able to get gas. They would eat off of what they had with them and keep driving.

"There isn't another town safe to stop in for another four or five hours' driving time." Kent folded the map back up and returned it to the glove compartment. "Planning on staying in one of them for the night or sleeping on the road?"

"We'll look at the town and decide once we see it. I don't know. I'm leaning more toward staying on the road."

"Why don't you want to stay in a town?" she asked.

"Because I don't know what their needs are. They might want the truck, or they might want you. Remember what we told you. You're our wife."

"I wish," she mumbled. If Wyatt heard her, he didn't let on.

They stopped at the next little town and decided they could park in the old Walmart parking lot for the night. No one seemed the least interested in them except when they wanted to barter for gas and food.

They climbed in the back of the truck and set up the mattress with sheets and a blanket and climbed under the covers. Jessie shivered and complained about being cold. Kent moved in closer and wrapped an arm around her.

"Hell, Jessie, you're like a block of ice. Wyatt, squeeze in next to her. She's really cold."

Jessie breathed a sigh of contentment when Wyatt hugged up next to her on the other side. It felt so good to have them so close to her. She'd take being cold anytime if it meant having them surrounding her like this.

"Jessie, turn on your side and wrap and arm around Kent's waist. I'll hold you from back here and keep you warm."

Jessie curled around on her side and snuggled up close to Kent, wrapping her arm around his waist and nudging his neck with her nose.

"Damn, your nose is even cold."

Wyatt spooned her from behind. She could feel his warm breath on the back of her neck. It warmed things deeper inside of her. Her pussy gushed in hopes of relief from the constant barrage of sexual need. She hated to tell it *not a chance*, but she knew Wyatt. If he even thought she was getting her jollies out of being held by them, he would put an end to it. She had to play it safe and behave—for now.

Chapter Three

Early the next morning, Jessie woke with the unmistakable feel of a hard cock pressed against her ass. She froze, unsure of what to do. A change in her breathing must have alerted Wyatt she was awake.

"Don't move." Wyatt's voice held strain in it.

"What's wrong, Wyatt?"

"Just don't move for a minute, okay?"

Jessie all but held her breath in an effort not to move. She knew Wyatt was trying to regain control of himself. She felt a little ashamed at herself for wishing he wouldn't. Finally, after what felt like forever, he pulled away from her and rolled over.

"Get up and get dressed, Jessie. Now."

Jessie sighed and crawled to the end of the mattress before standing up and grabbing clothes to put on. She edged behind the makeshift screen and dressed. She could hear the men arguing over something and knew it would be about her. She hated when they did that. She hated that she was younger than they were, because no matter how old she got, they would always see her as a teenager.

"Jessie?" Kent's voice came from around the screen where she stood waiting for someone to tell her she was allowed to come out.

"Yeah, is it safe for me to come out of my corner now?"

Kent walked around the screen and looked at her with a sad smile. "It's not like that, Jess."

"It sure as hell feels that way." She pushed past him and walked around the screen to jump down from the truck.

She didn't even wait for Wyatt to help her this time. She didn't need their help or their pity. The parking lot around them was deserted except for the empty cars and a few turned-over carts. The sky above them, though mostly still dark, held the faint glow of the rising sun off to the east.

"We're planning on eating the canned sausages with crackers. They're stale but still safe to eat." Kent held out a can toward her.

She shook her head. "Thanks, but I'm not hungry. I'm still full from last night's peanut butter crackers." She walked around to the front of the truck and sat on the step up.

"Jessie, I'm sorry I snapped at you this morning." Wyatt stepped in front of her.

She sighed and looked up with her best *I don't give a fuck* look. He didn't leave. Instead, he crouched down beside her and looked her in the eyes.

"Look, we've got a hard journey ahead of us. One that I honestly don't know how it's going to end. We can't afford to complicate things with sex."

"With sex. You think this is all about sex? That the way you treat me like a twelve-year-old is okay? It's not just about sex, Wyatt. You're the one with sex on the brain. It's about more than that. When you figure it out, come see me." She jumped up and walked off, making him fall back on his ass.

She walked back to the trailer, knowing better than to get too far away from the truck. They just didn't understand that she needed to feel like she meant something to them and wasn't just a burden they were bearing. She wanted someone to hold her sometimes, just because. Yeah, she wanted them. She was a full-blooded woman, but that wasn't all it was about. And Wyatt was old enough to figure it out.

Kent walked back to where she'd leaned against the trailer and leaned back next to her. Since they were the closest in age, he seemed to get her a little better, but still, in this, he was clueless.

"What gives, Jessie?"

"Nothing, Kent. Just let it go."

"We're going to be leaving in a few minutes, if you need anything from the back."

"I'm good." She continued to stare out over the dead town, wishing for the millionth time that she had died with her parents.

People were right. Dying wasn't so bad. It was the living that took guts.

"Come on, you two. We need to get on the road," Wyatt called back.

She stood up and headed for the front passenger side of the big U-Haul. She wondered if they would stop anywhere today other than to get gas. She grabbed the map as soon as she was settled in the cab and studied it.

"What are you looking for?" Kent asked.

"Show me where we are." She shoved the map into his lap.

He opened it and pointed to a circle. "Right here.

She checked their progress from Holly Bluff and decided they might make it to one of the salvaging locations late that afternoon. She wanted to get a few things if she could find them.

* * * *

Kent felt bad for Jessie. She couldn't win for losing with Wyatt. She was a female, and she was only twenty-one years old. Wyatt was only four years older, but he was the man of the house, so to speak, and as such, carried the full load of responsibility. He took it very seriously. What he didn't take was advice, at least not from his younger brother.

Jessie needed to feel less like a burden and more like a woman. He got that and tried to see her that way, but it was harder for his big brother to. Maybe once they got to where they were going to live, he would relax more around her. Kent hoped so, or they were going to have major issues soon.

He had seen Jess as a woman for the last five years. She had grown up fast and hard after her parents died, and the last two years had aged her both mentally and emotionally. Being constantly afraid someone would snatch you took a toll on a person. He supposed that was how important or famous people had always felt. He could almost see now why they did drugs and were so promiscuous. The pressure had to have gotten to them.

Well, the pressure was beginning to get to Jessie. Kent could see it, but Wyatt refused to see it. He was going to have a hell of a time when she finally blew up. He hoped it wouldn't prove to be dangerous. He had no idea what to expect ahead of them. David had told them as much as he knew, but that wasn't a lot, and they were going to be driving into the Border Lands themselves.

They stopped once at a gas station a little after two and filled up, trading the rest of their now-thawing food for the gas and some snacks. Jessie still didn't eat much, but Kent figured she'd make up for it that night. She usually didn't eat much when they drove, anyway.

Wyatt talked a lot more than usual on the drive. He pointed out places they might have once wanted to visit and talked about the next stops along the way. Jessie ignored him for the most part. Kent didn't think his brother was trying to draw her out, but he was definitely frustrated by her lack of participation.

Around six, they pulled into a Super Kmart store parking lot and drove around to the back where the loading dock was located.

"Do you see anything?" Wyatt asked no one in particular.

"I don't." Kent craned his neck around, but nothing seemed to move.

"It will be full dark soon. Let's camp here and then get an early start in the morning," Wyatt decided.

They started to climb out of the truck when Wyatt yelled for them to stop. Kent already had one foot on the ground with Jessie's ass in his face.

"Don't move," Wyatt said.

"What is it?"

"Wolf. It's watching you. Don't move."

Kent rested his head on the back of Jessie's ass. She was in a precarious position with one foot hanging off the running board. He used his head on her ass to give her a little support. He could tell her grip on the bar above her was weakening.

"Wyatt?" he asked.

"Just a minute. Let me get around there with the gun. Then we can move toward the building together."

Kent waited, hoping Wyatt hurried up. He was getting tired now, and not being able to see the wolf wasn't helping his sense of safety one iota.

"Okay, I've got him in my sights. Let's walk over to the stairs up to the landing. Move real slow."

Kent dropped his other foot to the ground and helped Jessie down after him. When they turned around, he heard Jess gasp. Only about fifty yards from them stood two wolves. Their mouths were open as they panted. He didn't think he'd been this close to one, other than in a zoo behind a cage.

"Okay, let's all walk very slowly to the stairs over there." Wyatt led the way.

Once they had climbed up to the landing, the wolves moved closer and sniffed around the truck but didn't try to follow them.

"They're probably just curious," he pointed out.

"Curious or not, I'd rather they go back where they came from," Jessie said.

"I think they live here." Wyatt tried the door and found it locked.

"What about one of the loading bay doors?" Kent suggested.

"You hold the gun, and I'll climb over and check on them." Wyatt handed the rifle to Kent before climbing over the railing and stretching over to the first loading bay.

He fiddled with the handle but couldn't make it move. He climbed over to each of the four bays, but all of them were locked from the inside. He made his way back to the landing and took the gun back from Kent.

"What about using the crowbar to open this door?" Jessie asked.

"Crowbar is in the truck. We're not," Wyatt pointed out.

"Duh, you have a gun, go get it. David said if we were careful and didn't move too fast, they would leave us alone."

"I don't like leaving you here without the gun while I'm scrounging in the back for the crowbar."

"So leave it with Kent, and he can cover you and us at the same time."

Kent looked at Wyatt and smiled. Wyatt grimaced but handed over the rifle to him. He waited until the wolves had made the complete circle of checking out the truck before he climbed down the stairs and walked slowly toward the truck.

"You're fine, Wyatt. They haven't moved. Just keep going." Jessie kept a constant soft dialogue going.

Kent didn't know if it was for her peace of mind or to ease Wyatt's worries, but it sure made him feel better. Once Wyatt had the crowbar, he started back. The wolves began to pace some when he was halfway across the parking lot. Kent used the railing to steady his hand with the rifle in case he needed to shoot. Right now, he was getting a little worried with how the wolves were moving around.

"Wyatt, they're beginning to pace back and forth. Should you stop for a while, or keep going?" he asked.

"I'm going to keep going. If they start toward me, fire a shot in front of them."

"Gotcha, brother." He drew a bead on the front paw of the lead wolf, just in case.

Wyatt made it to the stairs without them charging. Everyone let out a breath.

"Keep the rifle, Kent. You've got them covered. I'm going to pry open the door. If they start toward us, shoot them."

Jessie moved back against the railing to give Wyatt room while Kent kept a close eye on the wolves. He wasn't about to take his eyes off of them as long as they were a threat. He felt the heat from Jessie's body against his back. She probably didn't have much room, but he didn't want to change position now that he was set.

"Okay, got the door unlocked. I'm going to check it out. Stay here."

Kent didn't move, but Jessie's body heat disappeared from his back.

"Jessie?"

"I'm right here. I just moved over to give you more room."

After what felt like thirty minutes passed, Wyatt returned with a flashlight and motioned them all to come inside.

"It's set up like all Kmarts are, and there are skylights, so we'll have plenty of light in the morning. Until then, I guess we're going to be sleeping in here for the night. I'm not chancing the wolves tonight. We can't see them in the dark, and the sun is going down."

"What are we going to sleep on?" Jessie asked.

"There are air mattresses over in the sporting goods, I'm sure. We can blow one up and sleep on it." Wyatt smiled and hugged her as if he couldn't help it, then quickly let her go. "Let's head in that direction."

Kent shoved a crate over in front of the door to keep it closed and followed Wyatt and Jessie through the dark warehouse part of the store to the actual retail floor area. Kent kept the rifle pointed toward the ceiling but kept a lookout for any movement around them. In the dark, with only the flashlight and a faint glow from above, everything seemed to move.

When they arrived in the sporting goods area, Wyatt located a king-size air mattress and pulled it out of the box. It required a foot pump not included. Jessie located a foot pump and they took turns pumping up the mattress for the next twenty minutes. Once it was filled, Jessie grabbed a couple of sleeping bags and zipped them together to form a large cover for them.

"Ground rules. No wandering off in the middle of the night for any reason. Jessie, if you need to go to the bathroom, wake one of us up, and we'll go with you," Wyatt said.

"I think I can hold it till morning," she said, voice thick with sarcasm.

"Let's get some sleep, and we'll get an early start in the morning."

Kent removed his shoes but left his clothes on. Wyatt had made it clear they would remain dressed around Jessie at all times now. Sleeping in his clothes sucked.

Not long after they had all settled in for the night, the wolves outside began to howl. It made an eerie noise inside the silent store with its high ceilings. Kent felt Jessie shiver. He sighed and grabbed her hand to hold it. She dropped her head against his shoulder. It wasn't long before she was asleep.

"Wyatt?" Kent whispered.

"Yeah."

"Having no privacy to jack off is getting old, man."

"Tell me about it. But we aren't starting a relationship with her until we get somewhere to settle down. We've got to be alert, and sex makes you sloppy."

"Well, lack of sex makes you sloppy as well. I can't stop thinking about how much I want to fuck her."

"Kent, get a grip on your fucking cock. She's not just a place to put your dick, man."

"I know that. I'm just saying, is all. I've already told you I love her. I have for the last two years. You're the one who refused to let me court her."

"Court her? Is that what it's called now? I just thought you wanted to fuck her."

Kent sighed and blew out a breath in exasperation. Wyatt was going to drive him crazy about Jessie. He knew how he felt about her. If Wyatt wasn't sure, that was his problem. He could love and take care of her without his help. It was his loss.

Chapter Four

Wyatt woke first the next morning and found Jessie plastered to his chest with one leg between his legs. Fuck. He stood a good chance of getting racked, depending on how he woke her up. He lay there for a few more minutes, letting her scent wash over him. It wasn't that he didn't love Jessie. He did. He just wasn't sure it was the kind of love that having a sexual relationship would build on, or if it would tear them apart.

He knew his brother loved her. He didn't doubt that he knew his own mind, but he just wasn't sure a three-way relationship would work. There were times when he wanted Jessie so badly he hurt, but he wasn't sure if that were because it was Jessie or just because he was horny and she was available. She didn't deserve that. Neither did he.

It was still dark in the building, but he could just make out a faint light beginning to slide in the overhead skylights. It wouldn't be long before they would be able to see without the flashlights.

Jessie moved her arm and curled it around his neck. Then she hummed and rubbed her nose on his shirt. He waited, thinking she might be awake, but then the soft snore that was uniquely Jessie told him she was still asleep.

His cock stirred, feeling the warmth of her body against his. He willed it to cooperate, but it roared to life. He needed her off of him. Maybe even the knee to the nuts would help at this point.

"Jessie?" he whispered. "Wake up, baby. It's time to get up."

She stirred and yawned against his chest. Then she stilled, and he knew she was awake.

"Um, Wyatt?"

"Just be real careful moving your knee, Jessie. It's all good."

She rolled off of him without doing any lasting damage. He sighed and sat up, wincing at the kink it put in his cock.

"It's still dark," she complained.

"Going to be light in another thirty minutes or so. Thought you might like to get a head start in the bathroom."

"Yeah, sure. What about Kent?"

"Wake him up. He needs to go with us."

Jessie woke Kent up with a pop on the shoulder. "Wyatt said wake up."

"Shit, what time is it?" Kent grabbed the flashlight by his side of the mattress and turned it on.

"Let's head to the bathrooms and hope the water works." Wyatt picked up the other flashlight and grabbed a third he'd set up with a battery the night before.

"Can we stop by the housewares and pick up some towels and bath cloths? I'd like to take a spit bath if I can." Jessie took one of the flashlights from him.

"Good idea." He shone the light upward to locate the housewares department.

They grabbed clothes and towels and headed toward the sign that signified restrooms. He checked out the women's first to be sure it was safe before letting Jessie in and leaving her. He and Kent went to the men's bathroom to clean up.

Naturally, they were finished before Jessie. They looked around the immediate area, waiting for her to finish. When she finally came out, she looked much better. There were still circles under her eyes, but she wasn't as pale, and she seemed well rested. Wyatt hoped she would eat more, as well. She would lose weight at the rate she was going if she didn't eat more.

"Okay, I think the store is relatively safe. Don't go in any closed-up areas at all. Stay in the open, and we'll meet back up here as soon as our carts are full. There are plenty around here, so just grab one."

"I'll take the hardware section," Kent said.

"I'll start in the pharmacy area." Jessie grabbed the closest cart and took off.

"I'll stick here in the sporting goods. Shout out of you need anything," he called to Jessie.

"Sure," she called back, already halfway across the store.

Wyatt grabbed a cart and filled it full of hunting gear. All the guns and ammo were already gone, but there were a few knives left and plenty of other things they might need. He added all the Sterno that was on the shelves, along with a Coleman stove and cooking utensils. By the time he was finished, Kent had returned with a load of tools, rope, chains, and other hardware-type items.

"Where's Jessie?" he asked, looking at Kent.

"I don't know. She'll be here in a minute. You know how women are when it comes to shopping."

"Very funny, Kent." Jessie pushed a cart into the open area and pulled another one behind her.

"What in the hell do you have in all of that?" Wyatt asked, shaking his head.

"Soap, shampoo, deodorant, combs, brushes, toothbrushes." She picked up a box of tampons and wiggled it at them.

"Fine. What's in the other cart?" Wyatt pointed at the one she was pulling.

"Clothes and boots. I figure I'll need some heavier clothes and boots if we are going to be living in the wilds of the Border Lands. David said it was best to settle in the northern area and not in the plains area, because of the storms."

"She's got a point. We need to get some boots and warmer clothes too," Kent pointed out.

"Okay, let's load this stuff up first and see if our friends are still around."

They followed him as he led the way through the back, using the flashlights since there were no skylights in the back. After pulling the crate away from the door, Wyatt took the rifle and slowly opened the door. Then he stepped outside. He stuck his head back in the door and gave the all clear.

"I'm going to open one of the bay doors to let in light, and it will be easier to load the stuff up from it," Kent said.

Wyatt had Jessie stay in the doorway as he unhitched the trailer and backed the truck up to the loading bay Kent had rolled up. They spent the next thirty minutes packing away their supplies before going back for more. This time, they raided the grocery aisles and the home goods.

Once they were completely loaded and had shut everything back, they climbed in the cab of the truck and pulled out of the Kmart parking lot and back into town.

"Hey, Wyatt. We need to stop at a library," Jessie suddenly said.

"A library? Why in the hell would you want to do that?"

"We need some books if we're going to try and live off the land. There's a set called the Foxfire books. They talk about everything from how to make soap to how to put up vegetables. I'm going to need to know how to do all that."

"That's a good idea." Kent patted her on the knee.

Wyatt realized she was right and stopped the truck to figure out how to find a library. He decided their best bet was to grab a phone book from somewhere and see what street it was on and then look at the city map in the back.

As they headed for the first place they saw that might have a phone book, Kent laughed and pointed out a library across the street from them. Wyatt shook his head and pulled out front. He jumped out and locked the door, then waited for the others to follow suit. He scanned the area for anyone or anything that might be a problem, but other than the song of birds and the light wind blowing from the east, nothing stirred.

They had to break into the library and use the flashlights to see. They followed Jessie as she located the books they needed.

"You know. It wouldn't be a bad idea to grab several how-to books," Kent suggested.

Wyatt agreed with them. They took a rolling cart from the back of the library and filled it full of books on things such as carpentry, engine repair, growing vegetables, and even animal husbandry. Jessie added several first aid books as well. They rolled their books out to the truck and loaded them in the trailer. Kent took the cart back and closed the door back to the library so that it wouldn't just hang open.

"I'm good for something, now aren't I?" Jessie pointed out to Wyatt.

"I never said you weren't, Jess. I never said you weren't."

* * * *

Jessie sighed and closed her eyes as they pulled out of the little town. She'd eaten a good breakfast of canned fruit, but it wasn't sitting well with the driving. She just didn't ride well. She wondered if she would ride better if she tried to read. Maybe she would grab one of the books to look at when they stopped again.

The men talked about the map and where they were. She wondered how far they would get that night. She shut them out and thought about what life was going to be like when they settled down. David had said they would need to find an existing house somewhere and set up housekeeping in it and start a garden as soon as possible.

She knew next to nothing about gardens. She was a fairly good cook, but she didn't know how to cook fresh foods as much as canned or frozen food. Then there was the wild game the men kept talking about killing. She knew you had to cook it special. She needed to be reading those books now, while they were on the road.

They pulled into a small town about four hours later for gas and to eat. The people there were very curious and seemed to enjoy talking to them. Wyatt was naturally leery of them, so they didn't stick around long. She talked Kent into letting her get one of the books out of the back. They pulled back out on the highway and ate beef jerky and drank water as they drove.

"Why didn't you want to stick around there and eat?" she asked Wyatt.

"They were too interested in what we had in the back. I didn't trust they wouldn't try something."

Jessie shrugged and began reading the first book from the Foxfire set. By the time they were ready to stop for the night, she was on information overload. She never knew there was so much to living off the land. And she was only on the fifth chapter of the first book. At this rate, she'd need another three weeks of reading time to finish them. She wouldn't survive that long. She wasn't doing so well, as it were. She couldn't eat much while they rode and then didn't have much of an appetite when they stopped.

The truck stop they pulled into actually had a light on inside. Kent cautioned Jessie to lie down in the seat until they knew what was what. She lay with her head in Kent's lap and her ass next to Wyatt's.

"I'm going to pull up at the gas pump and then go inside and see what they'll trade for gas. You two stay here. Kent, keep the rifle at the ready. You know what to do if something happens."

Jessie didn't like the sound of that. She kept down and silent as Wyatt climbed out of the cab of the truck.

"What's going on, Kent?"

"He's walking inside right now. There's movement inside, but I can't see how many are in there."

"Do you think Wyatt will be okay in there alone?"

"He'll be fine. Here he comes now."

The door opened again and Wyatt climbed in. "Got to pull around to the other pumps. These don't work."

He cranked the truck and Jessie felt them move. She could see the awning above them as they circled around the building.

"Jessie, there are three men in there. No women that I saw. Don't stick your head up for anything. Do you understand?"

"I won't." She had no plans to be snatched again. "What are they going to trade for?"

"They need toilet paper and a drill. We've got lots of both and can probably get more." Wyatt climbed out of the truck and left her alone with Kent once again.

"Does everything look okay, Kent?"

"So far. He's filling the truck up now. One of the men is standing at the door, but inside, not outside."

"I don't feel good about this at all, Kent. Give me the handgun, and you keep the rifle close. Something's wrong."

Kent had learned a long time ago to heed her feelings. She seemed to have a sixth sense about things like that. She sighed when he reached beneath him and handed her the handgun and pulled the rifle up closer to the window.

"Can you tell Wyatt?"

"I'm going to try. Be very quiet. I'm going to roll the window down."

She watched him switch the key and then roll the window down. He leaned his head out the window and called over to Wyatt.

"Wyatt."

"Yeah, what do you need?"

"I want something from the store, come over here when you finish."

A few minutes later, Wyatt stepped over to the window, and Kent looked down at him.

"Jessie says something is wrong. You know how she can sense things. Be very careful," Kent whispered to his brother.

"Gotcha."

"What's going on now?" she asked a few seconds later.

"He's finished filling the tank and is carrying a box of tissue and the drill over to the door."

"Looks like everything is okay. They took it and waved him off."

Jessie sighed and relaxed. Then Kent cursed and yelled at Wyatt.

"Gun!"

She heard his rifle go off and then a second gunshot. She rose up with her gun at the ready and found Wyatt heading for them, holding his shoulder. Fuck, he'd been shot. She scrambled over to the driver's seat and cranked the truck up. She pulled over between him and the door so that Kent could pull him into the truck when he got there. Then she hit the gas and headed for the highway.

"What in the hell did I tell you to do if something like this happened?" Wyatt was yelling at Kent.

"You said to drive like a bat out of hell, and only a woman can do that, so I let her drive."

"This isn't funny, Kent."

"Fucking be quiet!" she screamed at Wyatt. "Let Kent see about your arm and shut up. I can't drive with you yelling."

Wyatt looked at her with his mouth open, then shut it and frowned. She glanced over as Kent tore Wyatt's shirt and exposed the wound. It looked like a trench had been dug through his arm, but the bullet hadn't lodged inside it, thank God.

"He's going to need stitches, but we'll have to stop for that," Kent said.

"We're not stopping until we have to stop for more gas," Wyatt said in a growl.

"Tie something around it to stop the bleeding, and we'll see what comes up next." She concentrated on driving.

She had to occasionally go around a deserted car, and that took all her ability with the trailer they were pulling behind them. At least with driving, she didn't feel sick anymore. Maybe Wyatt would let her drive some.

Two hours later, they drove into the outskirts of what looked like a small community. There were actually people walking around in the streets.

"What do you think, Wyatt? Can we stop here so I can sew you up?" she asked.

"Do you see any women?" Wyatt asked.

"I don't see any," Kent told them.

"Neither do I."

"Drive, then. We'll find a deserted place, and you and Kent can switch out driving and you can sew me up while he drives." Wyatt had his head leaned back against the back of the truck.

"I hate this."

"What, baby?" Kent asked.

"You can't stop when you need to because of me."

"It's not your fault, Jess. It's just that men are pigs," Kent told her.

"Tell me about it." Jessie flexed her hands on the steering wheel to ease the cramps in her fingers from gripping it so tightly.

They drove another hour and found a small, empty-looking town that boasted one grocery store. Wyatt agreed it looked safe enough, and they stopped. Kent climbed out of the truck and ran around the to the driver side and climbed back in. Jessie pulled out the first aid kit they'd put together for such an occasion and pulled out the antiseptic and the suture packet. She poured the medication on a cloth and cleaned the wound while Wyatt cursed a blue streak.

"Kent, get on the fucking road. We don't need to be still."

"Wyatt, I'll do better if we aren't moving."

"Drive, Kent. You'll do fine, Jess. Just sew me up."

Jessie grimaced and finished cleaning the wound. Then she tore open the sutures and bit her lip as she made the first stick. By the time she'd made six neat stitches, she'd bit a sore on her lower lip, and Wyatt was hoarse from cursing. She handed him some painkillers and a bottle of water. He swallowed them and drank half the bottle of water before he put it back down.

"I'm sorry, Wyatt. I tried not to hurt." There were tears in her eyes now that she didn't need to see anymore.

Wyatt leaned his head back and grabbed her hand and squeezed it.

"You did well, Jessie. It's all right to cry. I won't think you're weak, because you just sewed me up without shedding a tear when you had to be strong."

Jessie leaned her head back and let the tears flow. Hurting him had just about torn her apart inside. It didn't matter that it had to be done. She hated having to be the one to do it.

Chapter Five

Kent drove them into the night until they needed gas again. They stopped at a deserted little town that was on David's map. The gas station, however, wasn't deserted. An older woman and man stepped out of the door and watched them when they pulled up. The man walked over with his hands out as if to show he wasn't armed, but the woman had a shotgun.

Kent rolled down his window at the man's request.

"I'll pump your gas for you. What do you have to trade?"

"What are you needing?" Wyatt asked around Jessie.

"Got any ammunition?"

"Some, not a lot of that around."

"We need shotgun shells."

Wyatt looked at Kent who nodded slightly and looked down at the floorboard.

"How much to fill this truck up?"

"Box of shells."

"Sounds good to me. Go ahead and fill her up." Wyatt reached down and pulled up two boxes of shells.

"Hey, he said one," Jessie said.

"We don't have a shotgun, and they are being nice. I say give them both boxes."

Jessie shrugged.

Kent watched the man fill up the tank. He kept the truck running in case they needed to run. He felt pretty good about these people. They were up-front with the shotgun, and there was a woman.

Nothing said a woman couldn't be a thief, but he didn't get that feeling with this one.

"Okay, you're filled to the brim," the man said.

Kent handed over the two boxes of shells. "Keep the change," he said with a smile.

"Hey, thanks. Oh, wait a minute."

He ran over to his wife and showed her the two boxes of shells. She grinned and waved at them. The man disappeared inside the station then reappeared with a handful of something. When he got back around to Kent's window, he held up three homemade apple pies.

"Thanks!" Kent told him, and waved at the woman.

"What do you think? Should we try them?" Wyatt asked.

"Yeah, they smell delicious." Kent took a bite out of his and hummed his appreciation.

Jessie took a small bite of hers but didn't eat all of it. Kent was beginning to get worried about her.

"Not hungry?" he asked.

"I just can't eat when we're driving. I'll eat it when we stop for the night."

"That shouldn't be long now. We've got gas. The next place that looks safe, pull over, Kent. We all need rest tonight." Wyatt held his injured arm against his chest.

They found a small roadside park that was empty and decided to camp there for the night. Kent and Jessie pulled the back doors open and helped Wyatt climb up in the back. Kent added the handgun and the rifle to their bed. Then he sat up and cradled the rifle in his lap.

"We need to take turns staying awake from now on, I think," he said.

Wyatt nodded and sighed. "You're right. I'll take the next watch. I'm not much good to anyone right now."

Kent looked over at Jessie and winked at her. He would wake her up next and let her take watch. She needed to feel useful, and she was a damn good shot. She'd do fine.

He leaned against the side of the truck and kept an ear open as well. He was still running on adrenaline, so he was fine to stay up for several more hours before he would even be able to sleep. Jessie cuddled up close to Wyatt, who put his uninjured arm around her and didn't complain for once.

Three hours later, Kent woke Jessie up and traded places with her. He moved closer to her to keep Wyatt from hugging him. The man had gotten used to having Jessie next to him, he thought with a smile. *I figured he would fall asleep without any trouble.* But he kept thinking about the shooting and wondering what he would have done if Wyatt had been in worse shape.

Wyatt had told him to take Jessie and run if anything like that happened to him, but Kent couldn't see leaving his brother behind. He was sure his big brother wouldn't have left him. They were all three in this together. He wasn't leaving anyone behind.

Jessie was losing weight, and that bothered him as well. They had only been on the road three, going on four, days, and she had lost enough that her jeans were loose on her. She'd eaten the rest of the apple pie, but nothing else. She needed to eat better than that. He needed to work on her and get Wyatt on board.

Kent closed his eyes, and the next thing he knew, Jessie was waking him up at dawn.

"Wake up. I don't want to be the one to wake Wyatt up."

"I'm with you. Did you stay up all night? I meant for you to wake me up after a few hours." Kent yawned and stretched.

"I couldn't have slept if I wanted to. I was wide awake when it was time to change, so I just stayed up. I'll sleep in the truck some."

Kent sighed and reached over to wake Wyatt up. He was hot to the touch. Fuck.

"Jessie, feel Wyatt. I think he has a temperature."

Jessie reached over and felt of his forehead. "Yeah, he has. Wyatt, wake up." She shook him.

"What?" He rolled over on his bad arm and cursed before sitting up. "What's wrong?"

"You've got a temperature. You need to take something for it." Jessie handed him a bottle of water and two pills.

"What time is it? No one woke me up for watch."

"You had a fever. You couldn't take watch like that," Jessie told him, looking at Kent.

Kent got the message and nodded at him. "You wouldn't have been able to stay awake with a fever, and you might have missed something."

"So you've been up all night. I was going to let you drive." Wyatt frowned.

"No, Jessie took watch the rest of the night. I'll drive and you two can sleep."

"You let Jessie—"

"I am a damn good shot. I can take watch just as well as you two can, so don't say something you're going to regret." Jessie slammed her hand on the side of the truck before jumping down.

"Hey, wait up, Jess." Kent walked up next to her.

"What?"

"You need to eat more than you're eating." He tugged on her pants. "Your clothes are getting loose."

"I told you, I can't eat when we're driving."

"But you can eat now while we get ready. Go eat a can of peaches or something." He watched her stomp off and turned his back to give her some privacy to pee.

Once they were on the road again, Kent noticed Wyatt studying Jessie while she slept. He sighed and turned to look out the passenger side window.

"What is it, Wyatt?"

"Nothing."

"Not working this time, brother. What gives?"

"She's so damn feisty. How are we going to keep her safe if she doesn't mind us?"

"She does when it matters, Wyatt. Since we've been on the road, she's done just about everything we've asked her to do. She pushes our limits because she's a woman feeling confined but neglected."

"You been reading all those relationship books again?" Wyatt asked.

"She's made up her mind that she wants us, but we're ignoring her for the most part. When we aren't ignoring her, we're telling her what she can't do. We aren't giving her anything positive at all."

Wyatt rubbed his face with his good hand.

"Just think about it some, Wyatt."

Kent let his brother stew awhile before he brought up the fact they were getting closer to their destination and needed to decide where to put down roots. The last stop on the map was a place called Barter Town. They were supposed to get garden seeds, water, a map of the area, and keep Jessie hidden. Kent wasn't too keen on stopping there, since David said it was a stop off for female black-market traders. He didn't want to risk Jessie at all, but they needed the seeds. They also needed to gas up.

Jessie woke up about the time he pulled into a gas station marked on the map as a trade spot. He urged her to stay down while he negotiated their gas. Wyatt placed a hand on her head and stroked her hair. Kent wondered if he even realized he was doing it.

"Hey there, son," an older man with a bald head said, walking out of the building.

"Sir, we need to barter for some gas. What do you need?"

The man reached in his front shirt pocket and pulled out a piece of paper and handed it to him.

"Got any of this?" he asked.

Kent read over the list and smiled. He had just the thing. He handed the list back to the old man and said he'd be right back. He walked back to the trailer and unlocked the door. Inside was a set of metric screwdrivers. The man was looking for two or three. He'd give him the entire ten-piece set for a fill-up and something to snack on.

The old man's face lit up like a Christmas tree at the sight of the set. He agreed to fill up the truck and brought out some homemade bread and a small jar of peanut butter.

"I'd give you a knife, but I only have a couple, and we need them."

"We've got knives. Thanks for the bread. Haven't had any of that in a week." Kent watched as the old man worked the pump.

"Where you headed?"

"The Border Lands."

"Tough place. You've got to be able to live off the land out there. No electricity or anything. Gas trucks stop at Barter Town, and that's as far as they go, so don't drive farther than you can drive back to Barter Town," he advised.

"Thanks for the information and the gas and bread." Kent climbed back into the truck and they pulled back out on the highway.

"What was he saying?" Jessie asked as she rubbed her eyes.

"That the last gas stop is Barter Town. That means that we have about a sixty-mile radius we can drive to find a place to live and no further, or we won't be able to get back to Barter Town for gas," Wyatt told her.

"How far are we from there now?"

Kent looked at the map and grunted. "I'd say about ten hours. We can make it tomorrow. I would rather stop early tonight and get a good night's sleep and drive into Barter Town fresh."

"I agree," Wyatt said.

"How long am I going to have to ride in the back of the truck?"

"You're probably going to be back there for three or four hours by the time we barter for what we need and get on the road. We'll let you back up with us as soon as we're far enough away no one will see you." Wyatt winced when he bumped his arm.

"It's time for you to take some more meds, Wyatt." Jessie poured out two pills and handed them to him. "Let me look at your arm again, too, to make sure it's not infected."

He swallowed them with a couple of sips of water. Then he rolled up his sleeve so she could unwrap the bandage.

Kent winced at the reddened area on his brother's arm.

"Is it infected?" he asked.

"I don't think so. I think the low-grade fever and the slight redness are just the natural part of healing, according to the first aid books. Nothing is swollen and there isn't any drainage, so I think it is fine."

"Well, it still hurts, whether it's fine or not," Wyatt fussed.

"I didn't say it didn't," Jessie teased him.

Kent listened to them argue for the next thirty minutes. Then Jessie began reading in one of the books again. By the time he was ready to stop for the night, she'd nodded off, and Wyatt had grabbed the book so it wouldn't fall.

"How are you holding up with the driving?" Wyatt asked as he laid the book in his lap.

"Fine. I'll drive tomorrow, too."

"Tomorrow is going to be dicey. She has to stay in the back and be quiet. We can't afford for someone to see her."

"She will. She's afraid of being taken." Kent opened the door and turned to wake Jessie.

"Shhh, let her sleep until we have the mattress ready." Wyatt opened his door and climbed down.

Kent walked around behind the truck and unlocked the doors. He pulled the mattress to the edge and folded back the covers. He helped Wyatt climb up, then went back and got Jessie. She barely stirred when he picked her up and carried her to the back. She was exhausted. She'd stayed awake too much lately.

"I'll take first watch. Let's skip Jessie tonight. She needs to sleep." Kent covered her with the blanket.

"Sounds good to me. Just don't forget to wake me up, because I need you at your best tomorrow. I'm handicapped," Wyatt pointed out.

"I will. I'm tired from driving, so I'll be ready for you to spell me in a few hours."

"Is Jessie eating any better?" Wyatt asked.

"She ate more today than yesterday. She said she can't eat and ride. Riding makes her nauseous."

"I never knew that."

"I think there's a lot about her we don't know about."

Chapter Six

They pulled into Barter Town at nine the next morning. Jessie was in the back of the truck behind the mattress and divider they'd set up. She had plenty of cushions, so she could sleep if she wanted to. Wyatt wasn't worried about anyone finding her as long as she was quiet. He was much more worried that she would get too hot back there before they could get her back up front with them.

"Remember, in and out as fast as we can. Let's get gas first and then barter for the seeds next." Wyatt directed Kent toward one of the gas stations in the bustling town.

This was the first place they'd been that reminded him of a city before the catastrophes, as far as activity went. There were people everywhere. Well, men mostly. The few women he saw were actually tied or chained to their men. He saw an advertisement for a brothel. Hell, the place was like some horror movie.

Kent shook his head and pulled up at the gas pump. A man walked out to see what they wanted.

"What do you need?" Kent asked.

"Ha, don't need anything. Just depends on what you've got."

They came up against this with every transaction they made. It took them nearly three hours of hard bartering to end up with what they'd come for. They had seeds for a full vegetable garden, six cases of bottled water, and a map of the immediate area.

As soon as they were far enough out of town that they didn't worry about someone seeing them, Kent stopped the truck while Wyatt ran around and unlocked the back to let Jessie out. She emerged sweaty and shaking.

"Here, drink some water. Not too fast." She followed his directions and then accepted his help up into the truck.

"I'm sorry you were back there so long," Wyatt said.

"I'm okay, just hot."

"Let's look at the map and decide on a direction to go," Wyatt said. He opened up the map, and they looked it over.

"Looks like there are more roads going northwest than anywhere. That means more people and more places to live," Wyatt said.

"I agree to going that direction, but we need to draw a circle for how far out we can safely drive and be able to get back," Jessie said with a yawn.

Kent grabbed a pen and measured the length in miles using the key. He drew a circular area around the area in question. Wyatt looked over the area he'd circled and nodded.

"Okay, that gives us three main roads. Which road do you want to take?"

"Jessie? You choose. You usually have good instincts." Kent handed her the pen.

She drew in a deep breath and then let it out slowly. She studied the map and picked out a road.

Wyatt took the map and spread it out to see how they were going to get to the road she picked. It was a straight shot until they got about fifteen miles from the road, and then they would have a few turns to make. It looked as good as any, though.

He smiled at her and gave the map to Kent. "Let's get started. Looks like we have about a five-hour drive ahead of us."

"Jessie, you need to eat first. We aren't going anywhere until you get something in your stomach."

Kent handed her a hunk of the bread from the last place they'd stopped before Barter Town. Then he opened a can of pears. She ate the bread and half the pears. Wyatt managed the rest of the pears.

"Okay, let's get going. We've got about six hours of sunlight left. I'd like to find a place and clear it as safe before dark." Wyatt folded the map to where they were and the first fifteen miles.

"Maybe we will find a place that's fairly close," Jessie said.

"Remember, you stay down in the truck each time we stop to check a place out. We don't want anyone to see you," Wyatt reminded her.

"I understand." She smiled, but Wyatt could tell she didn't feel well. It worried him.

She'd lost weight, wasn't eating well, and was tired. It didn't make sense. What could be wrong with her? The idea that anything was wrong bothered him, but to not know what it was scared him. They didn't have doctors to go to out here. How could he take care of her if he didn't know what was wrong?

"Wyatt? Are we ready to go?" Kent looked at him funny.

"Yeah, let's head out."

They drove for a good four hours before they came to a road that led off the main road they were on. Kent took it, and they wound around for a good thirty minutes before they drove up into a clearing. Jessie immediately lay down on the seat as a house emerged from the trees. Wyatt patted her head and looked at the building in front of them. It was in need of repair but didn't look like it was in bad shape. There were no boards or windows missing. The roof looked sound, from what he could see.

"What do you think?" Kent asked.

"Let's check it out. Jessie, keep the handgun in your hand. We're going to look around. Keep the doors locked. We have a key to get in." Wyatt opened his door and slid out while Kent did the same on the other side.

He locked the doors and closed his after Kent shut his side. They each carried a rifle and eased up on the front door of the house. Wyatt knocked on the door and stood back. He repeated the knock when no one came to the door. They walked around the house and checked every window as they went. All of the doors and windows were locked. There was no car or truck in the carport or around the property.

"It's beginning to get dark. We need to check inside. Do you want to break a window or the door?" Kent asked.

"Look around for a key first. You never know." Wyatt began searching under stones, the doormat, and flower pots.

Kent shouted in triumph, holding up a key. "In the mailbox, at the bottom."

They unlocked the house and walked inside. It smelled musty, but there wasn't an odor as if anything had died in the house. That was good. It would have been hard to get rid of the smell. Wyatt searched for anything dangerous and found nothing. Kent checked all the upstairs while he checked the downstairs. He found a door that led into a cellar, but without a light, he couldn't check it out. He would do that later with the flashlight. It smelled musty, like the house. Kent walked down the stairs and joined Wyatt in the living room.

"What do you think?" he asked.

"I think it's a good bet. It's clean, no structural damage, and there's plenty of cleared land around it for a garden. There are even a couple of out buildings. One of them can be a barn." Kent shrugged.

"Think Jessie will like it?" Wyatt asked.

"Yeah, I think she will."

"Let's go get her and the flashlights." Wyatt led the way out to the truck.

Jessie stuck close to them as they showed her the house. She was obviously scared. That bothered Wyatt. He didn't want her always afraid. She seemed to like the house fine, though.

Kent asked, "What next?"

They both looked at Jessie for the answer.

* * * *

"We make a plan. I need paper and a pen and the flashlight." Jessie walked over to the kitchen table.

Kent rummaged around and found a pen that worked and some scratch paper in a drawer. He handed it to Jessie, and they waited as she made out a list.

"First thing is we need to bring the mattress in and put it in the middle of the living room floor for tonight. We'll sleep there and then get up in the morning and clean. The kitchen, a bathroom, and the bedroom are the three main rooms to be cleaned first."

"Okay, Kent, we have our marching orders. Let's clear out the middle of the living room floor."

Jessie watched them move the living room furniture around the edge of the room and then bring the mattress in. She helped as much as she could, since she was afraid Wyatt was going to burst his stitches. Somehow, they managed to get it in the room without that happening. She added the blankets and pillows and then checked the kitchen out.

The refrigerator was completely empty. Nothing was in it, as if the people who lived there had known they would be leaving. The cabinets were full of dishes, so they wouldn't need them. The stove was gas. When she turned the burner knob, it made a hissing noise, making her think that it still had gas going to it.

"Wyatt. Come here a minute," she called out.

Wyatt walked in carrying a case of water. He sat it on the counter.

"Listen." She turned the knob and the hiss began again.

"I'll be damned," Wyatt said. He rummaged around until he came up with a box of matches. "Move back in case it flares."

Jessie moved back and watched as Wyatt struck a match, then turned on the gas. The burner lit without a problem. She smiled and hugged him. He actually hugged her back.

"What's all the celebrating for?" Kent walked into the kitchen carrying a case of water.

"Look." She pointed to the gas stove.

"Wow. I wonder how long it will last?"

"Let's plan on it lasting forever and not borrow trouble," Wyatt said.

"How bad is the fridge?" Wyatt asked, looked at it warily.

"It's completely empty. Doesn't even smell. It's like the owners knew they were leaving."

"That's odd." Kent opened the door and looked inside. "Well, don't guess it really matters, since we don't have electricity."

"How much more do you plan to unload tonight?" Jessie asked them.

"Just the rest of the water and the seeds," Wyatt said. "Then we'll call it a night and get an early start in the morning."

She watched them carry everything in and then took the flashlight to check out the pantry. It was a fairly large room with lots of canned goods. There were some dead potatoes that had grown and died for lack of water, as well as onions. She'd have to clean their carcasses out. She found that they kept their flour, sugar, and cornmeal in plastic containers. She wondered if they were any good. There didn't appear to be any bugs in any of them. The sugar was a hard lump but could be broken down.

"What are you doing in there?" Wyatt asked her.

"I'm checking to see what all is in here. We've got a good variety of canned goods."

"We've got a small picnic set up in the living room. Come on and eat."

Jessie chuckled and followed Wyatt into the other room, where Kent was spreading peanut butter on the bread.

"Looks good to me." She took the piece of bread from him and took a bite.

"Hey!" He reached to grab it back, but she scooted out of his reach.

Wyatt laughed and sliced another piece and took the peanut butter away from Kent. The other man sighed and opened a can of pineapple and began eating it. They passed around more food and made a small feast. It was the most she'd eaten since they'd left Holly Ridge. It would be their first night in their new home, too. She was celebrating. Things would be fine now. They would all be a family. Wyatt would relax and not be so uptight now that they had a home. She'd give him a few weeks before she started pushing again. They did have a lot of work to do first.

"Okay, time for bed. We need to get up early in the morning and get to work." Wyatt helped Jessie clean up the food.

They put the bread in the refrigerator since it would be safe from bugs there, not that she had seen any since they'd been in the house. In fact, she couldn't remember seeing many bugs at all on the drive out of Barter Town once they'd put her up front with them. She was used to lots of bugs back home. If they didn't have them here, she'd be ecstatically happy.

They climbed onto the mattress fully clothed and pulled the cover up over them before turning off the flashlight and listening to the dark. Jessie was sure she'd never fall asleep in a strange place, but the next thing she knew, morning light was shining in the windows.

* * * *

"Hey, guys, it's morning." She shook Kent since she didn't want to hurt Wyatt's arm.

"Hmm?" Kent opened one eye and squinted at her. "Are you sure?"

"Silly." She crawled out of the covers and off the mattress.

Wyatt groaned and rolled over to look up at her. "You sure are chipper this morning."

"We have a new home. I can't wait to get to work on it."

"She's going to work us to death, you watch," Kent complained.

"Come on guys. If you find me the coffee, I'll boil up some for you."

That got Kent up and going. He scratched his head and then his chest like a typical male. Then he unlocked the front door and walked outside.

"Shut the door, its cold out there," Jessie complained when the cooler air hit her bare feet.

"Women, can't make 'em happy." Kent laughed and closed the door.

Wyatt finally climbed out of the covers and stood up. She launched herself at him and wrapped her arms around his waist.

"What?"

"I'm so happy. We have a home. It's going to be great."

"You need to realize it's going to be hard, too. We have to live without electricity, and garden and live off the land."

"I know, don't rain on my parade." She pouted.

He chuckled and patted her on the head. "Let's see about breakfast."

Kent walked back in with a tin of coffee and a giant smile on his face.

"What?" Wyatt and Jessie asked at the same time.

"There are deer eating in our backyard."

"Oh! I want to see!" She ran to the back door and peered through the window. Sure enough, a buck and two does grazed in their backyard.

"This could pose a problem for the garden," Wyatt said.

"Oh, I'm not worried. You'll have them on our dinner table before the garden comes up." Jessie smiled at them.

"I could do that now, if you want," Kent offered.

"Not till I've cleaned this kitchen well. It's dirty."

"What do you want us to do?" Wyatt asked.

"After we eat and have coffee, I want to drag all the furniture from the kitchen into the living room. Then you can bring in the box with the cleaning supplies. After that, you probably need to look around the house and see what there is around here. I can handle cleaning by myself. You need to see about the outside stuff while you have good light."

"Yes, ma'am," Wyatt said with a smile.

They fixed skillet toast after Jessie cleaned a frying pan and had toast and pears for breakfast. She watched as the men shoved the furniture out of the eat-in kitchen and pulled the fridge out from the wall so she could clean behind it. After they finished that, the men disappeared outside while she got to heating water to clean with.

Three hours later, she had a spotless kitchen and was busy working on the dining area. It felt good to be moving around doing something, and not stuck in the cab of a truck wondering what was ahead. As soon as she finished the dining area, she started on the pantry. She checked expiration dates and threw away lots of canned meat. Most of the veggies and fruit were safe. She cleaned cans, jars, and shelves. Her stomach rumbling reminded her it was past time to eat.

She walked out the back door to look for the men when a cow came meandering up to the porch and looked at her. She wasn't sure if it was dangerous or not, so she didn't move. Finally, after it realized she wasn't going to do anything, it walked farther into the yard.

"What are you doing?" Wyatt asked from inside the kitchen.

"Looking at this cow."

"What cow?" He walked outside and laughed. "I'll be damned. We have a cow."

Kent walked up. "That's not all we have. There's a fully functional horse barn over there." He pointed to the side where a building stood. "And there's another barn that must be for storing hay on the other side of the horse barn."

"So the people that lived here owned horses. What happened to them?" Jessie asked.

"All the stall doors were open, and the barn doors were as well. I'd say they let the animals out to run wild," Kent suggested.

"Why did they leave? Nothing is wrong here," Jessie wondered out loud.

"Could be that they got sick and left, or they couldn't handle not having electricity. There's not much telling," Wyatt said.

"Do you think they'll come back?"

Chapter Seven

"I think that if they were coming back, they'd have been back long before now." Wyatt smiled and rubbed her arm before turning back to look at the cow in the backyard. "Think we can herd it into the barn?" he asked Kent.

"I think so. Basically everything I've heard about cows is that they are dumb animals."

"Well, be careful, that dumb animal weighs three times more than you do." Jessie left them on the back porch.

"Any suggestions?" Wyatt asked.

"How about we just walk up to it and push it?"

"You want to push an animal that weighs about what a car weighs."

"Hey, you asked," Kent reminded him.

"Okay, go get some of that rope you stole and bring it back. We're going to rope it and lead it to the barn."

Kent returned with the rope, and Wyatt made a loop with it and approached the cow. It moved farther away. He tried again, and again the cow moved off.

Kent was beside himself laughing.

"Get over here and stand so that it won't go that way." Wyatt was fast getting exasperated.

The cow started to move off toward Kent, then thought better of it and tried to move forward. Wyatt looped the rope over its head and pulled it tight around the animal's neck. Then he pulled, and the cow pulled back.

"Fuck. This isn't working," Wyatt said.

"Let's try this." Kent walked to the side of the animal and popped it on the flank and yelled at it.

The cow moved in the right direction. They got on either side of it and popped and yelled until they had it in a stall in the barn.

"Now what do we do, farmer Wyatt?" Kent asked.

"Gather some grass and put it in the bucket for it to eat."

"Great, now I get to cut grass." He left Wyatt with the cow.

Wyatt laughed and walked back out to find Jessie petting a calf.

"Think this belongs to that in there?" she asked.

"Could be." Wyatt took the rope and put it over the neck of the calf and led it into the barn and put it in the stall with the cow. It immediately began sucking teat.

"Guess it does," Wyatt said when Jessie joined him looking over the stall door.

"Where's Kent?" she asked after a few seconds.

"Getting grass for the cow to eat."

"I bet he loved that."

"He was a little amused."

Jessie leaned in to Wyatt. He enjoyed the feel of her against him. He could smell the sweet smell of lemon for some reason.

"You smell like lemon."

"It's the cleaner I was using. Its lemon scented. It sure isn't me. I probably smell like a pig. I've been sweating, and in all sorts of dirt."

"More than likely Kent and I smell worse." He chuckled. "We're going to be glad for a bath tonight."

"That reminds me. You need to check to see if the hot water heaters are gas or electric. If they are gas, they need the pilot lights lit. If they aren't, we have to heat water for baths."

"Damn, things are so complicated." Wyatt shrugged. "I'll go check that now, because if we want a hot bath, the water needs time to heat up."

He left Jessie on the back porch sweeping and took the matches with the flashlight to the hot water heater in the basement. It was gas.

Thank God. He lit it and checked out the rest of the cellar. It had lots of cobwebs, but not much else. There were shelves where a few canned goods sat, but not many. Mostly, it was dirty.

He went upstairs and found the water heater for the bathrooms up there and lit it as well. When he came back downstairs, it was to find Kent kissing Jessie. He instinctively started to stop them, then realized there was no reason to anymore. They were in a safe place, the best that he could determine. He couldn't keep them apart forever. Not living with each other as they were.

Instead, he backed up and walked outside. He could admit to himself he was jealous more of not being a part of it than of his brother. He liked seeing them kissing. It had made him hard. Living with them together was going to be difficult at best, especially as much as he wanted her. But he couldn't ask her to be a wife and lover to two men. No matter what he and his brother had discussed at one time.

She deserved to be treated like a queen. He planned to be sure she had everything they could give her and make life as easy for her as possible. What was he thinking? Life here was going to be damn hard no matter what they did. She'd do fine, though, because she was strong.

"Hey Wyatt, what are you doing?" Kent asked.

"Looking out over the yard. The front needs some work, or it'll take over the house. We need to cut back as much as we can to let as much light in as possible. With no electricity, we're going to be relying on the sun."

"Wonder about getting solar panels to help with conserving energy by heating the house up. Otherwise, we're going to be sleeping in front of the fireplace all winter."

Wyatt nodded. Kent was right. They needed to be thinking about winter. It was already pretty damn cool in the mornings, and they were just getting into spring.

"I hate to say this, but I think we need to be making a list of things like Jessie does."

Wyatt tested the porch swing and found it solid. It would be nice to sit out here with her on a summer evening. He sighed. Only it wouldn't be him, it would be Kent. It was really better that way anyway. They were closer to the same age.

"Why the frown?" Kent asked.

"We need to talk about Jessie when she's busy somewhere."

"What about her?"

"Just stuff. Later." He got up and walked back in the house to find the woman in question polishing the kitchen table.

"How does it look?" she asked him.

"Looks good. You ready to put it and the chairs back in the dining area?"

"Yeah, thanks. Did you get the hot water heaters lit?"

"Yeah, we should have hot water for showers later."

"Then I better go clean a bathroom."

Wyatt watched her grab her little tray of cleaning supplies and head upstairs. The house had four bedrooms and three bathrooms, with a half bath downstairs next to the living room. There was a walk up over the garage that he hadn't explored yet. They had too many other things to do right now.

"Where is Jessie?" Kent asked, walking into the living room.

"Cleaning a bathroom. Come on and help me. She wants these put back in the dining area again."

"She sure has been busy today. She's going to sleep well tonight."

"I think we all will. How much grass did you get in the bucket for the cow?" Wyatt asked with a grin.

"Plenty. Where did the calf come from?"

"It walked up after you went to get the grass."

"You know what that means, don't you?"

"What?" Wyatt asked.

"Fresh milk."

Wyatt shook his head. Leave it to Kent to think about food.

"What did you want to talk about? She's busy now."

Wyatt drew in a deep breath and motioned for Kent to follow him outside.

"Look, we've found a home here, and I think we'll do fine. I know you've wanted to date Jessie for the last five years and all. I guess what I'm saying is, I'm not going to stand in your way anymore. She deserves to be happy, and I know you will make her happy."

"Um, Wyatt. She isn't going to be happy without you, too."

"I know we talked about making it a threesome, but Kent, that's asking too much of her."

"You're not asking her. She's accepting you. Don't hurt her and turn her away."

"I know you're not having this conversation without me."

Wyatt cringed. He hadn't heard her come up.

"Jessie, you and Kent have been eyeing each other for years. I'm not going to interfere anymore. That's all."

"But you don't want to be a part of it. Is that what you're saying?"

"No, I mean—damn it, Jessie. It won't work."

"What won't work? Our loving each other? The three of us caring for one another? I think it will." Wyatt stuck his hands on his hips.

"Wyatt, don't do this, man." Kent shook his head.

"How can you stand there and talk to me about fucking the woman you love? Doesn't it bother you at all, Kent?" Wyatt asked.

"It's not like you're some stranger I don't know. You're my brother, and I know that you love her and will take care of her if anything happens to me. Seeing her wrapped in your arms only turns me on." Kent pulled Jessie back against him.

"And what if seeing her in your arms just pisses me off?"

"Does it?" Kent asked.

Wyatt slapped his hand against the porch post and turned away.

"It doesn't, does it? That's what has you so upset. You like seeing her in my arms. You like the idea of making love to her with me."

Wyatt looked out over the backyard, trying to calm down. He needed to get control of his emotions to have this conversation with them. Hell, he'd only wanted to talk to Kent and settle it that way. Having Jessie in it only made it harder.

"Wyatt, I love you. Do you not love me?" Jessie's wrapped her arms around his waist.

He closed his eyes and tried to feel what was going on inside of him right then. Was it lust or love? He fucking didn't know. All he knew was that, yes, he wanted to fuck her. He wanted to watch his brother fuck her, but he didn't know if it was more than that or not.

"Jessie. I care about you. I don't know how I feel about you other than that."

She ran a hand down his abdomen and wrapped it around his cock through his jeans.

"Is this for me as someone you care about, or as a woman you want?" she asked.

Wyatt grabbed her wrist and pulled her hand away from his cock. It was one of the hardest things he'd had to do lately. Fuck, he wanted her.

"Come on, Jessie. Let's go see about that bathroom. I think Wyatt needs some alone time."

"Jessie—I'm sorry." Wyatt let go of her wrist and waited until they'd left the porch.

He felt like a hole had opened up inside and was swallowing him. He'd never told Kent about Leslie. He'd loved her more than anything the year he'd had at college before the catastrophes. It was as if they'd just clicked and were inseparable from then on. They had almost the same class schedule and were majoring in the same thing. He had really thought they would be together forever.

He hadn't said anything to his family about her because he wanted her all to himself for a while. He didn't want them harping about bringing her home and introducing her to them. He wanted to know everything about her before he did that. Then all hell broke loose, and he lost her.

One day she was there, and the next she wasn't. He had come back from a weekend at home to find that she hadn't come back to college. He'd called her cell and her home number only to get out of order messages. He finally found out that her hometown had been demolished by a tornado, and almost everyone had been killed.

He couldn't get any information about what had happened to her, and even when he made the trip there and witnessed the devastation, he continued to hold out hope she was alive somewhere, waiting on him to find her.

Several weeks later, their hometown was hit, and he found himself taking care of Jessie and his brother in a world that was fast changing course. Now he was being asked to be part of a ménage relationship, and he didn't know for sure that he loved Jessie the way she deserved to be loved.

Wyatt let out a long breath and walked out to the back of the yard to where the trees started. He studied the landscape without really seeing it. How were they going to survive in this new place if they were at odds with each other? He had to figure out how to make Jessie accept that he just wasn't sure how he felt, and not let it tear them all apart.

A movement in the woods caught his attention. He willed himself to be still and waited to see if it would happen again. For long moments nothing stirred, then a lone wolf walked into a shaft of sunlight that penetrated the wood's dimness.

Not good. He hadn't even considered that there would be wolves out here as well. Naturally there would be. It was their environment. He needed to warn the others to be careful and not go off alone anywhere. Even here, in their new home, there were unseen dangers to worry about.

He waited for the wolf to continue on its way before he backed away from the trees and returned to the house. They needed to have a family meeting and discuss the dangers and their next course of action. He and Kent had found a lot of equipment in the other outdoor building. He hoped it would be enough to get them started as a farm. They had about five months of warm weather left before winter hit. They needed to put aside the emotional crap and get to work.

Chapter Eight

"Jessie, he'll come around. Give him time. He's under a lot of pressure, being the oldest. It's bound to be affecting how he sees you. To him, right now, you're his responsibility, and he's always taken that very seriously." Kent pulled her into his arms.

She looked up into his eyes and knew she loved him, but she also knew she loved Wyatt as well. How could she handle being around and seeing Wyatt every day without being able to show him she loved him? It hurt deep inside of her.

Kent bent down and kissed her. He nipped at her lower lip until she opened to him, then delved inside her mouth where he teased her with his tongue. He licked the roof of her mouth and tickled along her cheek. She sucked on his tongue until he was fucking in and out of her mouth, much as her body ached for him to do to her pussy. She needed him.

"Kent?" she whispered.

"Soon, baby. Soon."

She let him hold her for a few more seconds, then pulled away and wiped the tears from her eyes. She had things to do. They had a lot to get done before winter. She wasn't helping matters by being needy.

"Let's see if you can fix this leak." She handed him the wrench and a small bag of washers.

"I think I can handle this. You go on and see which of the bedrooms we're going to clean up first."

Jessie left Kent working on the dripping faucet and checked each of the bedrooms. The best one for all of them was the master, where he was in the master bath now. It wouldn't be the easiest, as there was a lot of junk in that bedroom, but it made the most sense because it was directly over the kitchen where there would be some heat during the winter. Plus it was large enough for all of them.

The problem was, what about Wyatt? Would he continue to sleep with them, or would he demand his own room? She really didn't want to be separated from either of the men at all. Not just because she loved them both, but because deep down, she was still afraid she would be taken. She still had nightmares about it. She felt safer between them than she did with only one of them.

"Hey, Jessie? I think I have it fixed." Kent's voice called out from the bathroom.

Jessie walked back in and found him sitting on the floor next to the massive tub.

"See? No more leak." He turned the water on and then off, and it stopped dripping.

"Cool. One problem down."

"So, what bedroom?"

"I want us all to stick to the master because it's safer for us all to be together and it's the largest room."

"What about Wyatt?"

"He stays with us until he refuses to. Then he can fix his own damn room." Jessie huffed out a breath and walked out of the bedroom and downstairs.

She checked her watch and realized they would need to see about supper soon as it would be getting dark in another couple of hours. She rummaged around in the kitchen and came up with Spam that wasn't out-of-date and decided on fried Spam with green beans and pinto beans.

She had everything ready when the men showed up. They each looked preoccupied, so she kept her mouth shut, and they ate in silence. Once all the dishes were put up, they sat at the kitchen table and discussed their plans for the next few days.

"We don't have a lot of time until winter gets here. Kent and I found a garden tiller in the shed out back. We're going to work on it so we can till up a garden. Once we have it ready, Jessie, we need you to handle the planting and general upkeep while we work on other things. We'll till it when it needs it periodically," Wyatt began.

"I can do that. I'll also keep working on the house until I have it completely cleaned out. Then we'll move all of our stuff in it."

"Good deal," Wyatt said. "The other thing is that I saw a wolf in the woods this afternoon. Where there is one, there's a pack, so no one goes anywhere by themselves, and always carry a gun with you."

"Oh, God. I hadn't thought about there being wolves out here." Jessie shivered.

"We'll have to keep the cow and calf in the barn or close to the house," Kent said.

"I'd like to also get that fence repaired so we can let them out in that pasture some during the day. They can graze in it while we're working." Wyatt made a note on his pad.

"The master bathroom is clean and in working order. The master bedroom is next. Then we can move our own mattress upstairs to that bed."

"What other room is workable?" Wyatt asked without looking at her.

"I understand if you don't want me, Wyatt, but for now, at least, I need you to stay with us in the same room. I'll feel safer."

"Jessie, you're asking a lot of him," Kent began.

"That's okay, Kent. I'll stay with you, for now. She's probably right. We don't know anything about this place. It's better if we stick together. I'll give you plenty of alone time, if you're worried about that."

Kent just shook his head.

"So, you two are going to work on the tractor thingy and fix the garden the rest of this week while I work on the house. Is that the plan?" Jessie asked.

"That's the plan." Wyatt stood up and walked over to the stairs. "I'm going to take a shower and change clothes. I'll be down in about thirty or forty-five minutes."

Jessie figured that was his way of giving them some privacy. She smiled at Kent and stood up. "I'm going to get my bag out of the truck."

She didn't want Wyatt to know how much it hurt her for him to pull away like he was doing. She wasn't sure how she was going to handle losing that part of him. It didn't matter that she'd never really had it to begin with.

* * * *

Wyatt looked in the mirror in the fading light. He looked like hell. He ran his hands over his face and leaned against the sink. He needed to shave off the new growth of beard he had and cut his hair. He looked like a mountain man with his long, curly hair and wiry beard. Why would Jessie even want him?

He shook that thought off and turned on the shower while he pulled off his clothes. The warm water felt great to his parched skin. It had been a long week of spit baths. He quickly washed and rinsed off. He shampooed his hair and rinsed it out as well. Then he looked down at his swollen cock and closed his eyes. He couldn't go back downstairs with another hard-on to climb into bed next to Jessie.

Wyatt wrapped his hand around his thick cock and began tugging in long, slow pulls trying to summon a picture of Leslie in his mind. Try as he might, he couldn't picture her anymore. All he could see in his mind's eye was Jessie smiling up at him. He cursed and tugged harder. His balls were on fire with need.

Instead of Leslie on her knees with his cock in her mouth, he saw Jessie's pink lips stretched wide around his cock with love in her eyes as she swallowed him down her throat. He groaned and quickened his pace. He reached between his legs with his other hand and squeezed his balls. Lightning flashed down his spine as he felt the beginnings of his climax building. He cursed and let his mind think about Jessie.

Her heavy-lidded eyes would stare up at him as he fed his dick to her one inch at a time. She'd moan around him and suck his cock all the way to her throat and then swallow around him. He imagined holding her head as he fucked her mouth, her hot tongue gliding over his cock like a warm glove. With each pass of her lips over his shaft, he grew harder, if possible, as she let her teeth graze his cock.

He went up on his toes as the first shots of cum spewed from his hardened cock to splash against the ceramic tiles. He pulled faster and squeezed tighter as he came harder than he'd ever come before.

Wyatt leaned against the cool tile and gathered his strength to clean up and shut off the water. He needed to save some of the hot water for them. They would probably take a shower together. He cursed at the thought. Why was he being so stubborn about it? She said she loved him. Why wasn't that enough?

He just wasn't sure it was love, though, either for her or for him. He still thought about Leslie all the time, and even though he didn't love Leslie, he didn't know if how he felt about Jessie was more than just lust. It bothered him that he didn't mind that his brother was fucking her. It should bother him if he really loved her.

He dried off and dressed, then checked his watch. It had been nearly an hour. They were going to have to use the flashlight to take a shower. He grabbed up his dirty clothes and rushed down the stairs, only to stop in midstride when he got to the living room.

Jessie was totally nude.

* * * *

Jessie took Kent's cock deep in her throat as he face fucked her over and over. She moaned around him. Her hands found his balls and began to manipulate them, then scratched lightly over them with her nails. Kent hissed out a breath.

"I want you, Jessie. I want in that tight cunt. Get up and bend over the couch for me, baby."

Jessie immediately stood up and bent over the couch arm and looked back over her shoulder at him. He stroked her pussy with his cock, then lined it up with her slit and plunged forward. Jessie groaned as he shoved his way in until he reached the back of her. She could feel him bump her cervix and thrilled at the pleasure of it.

He pounded into her over and over, pulling almost all the way out before tunneling back in with his massive cock. She wanted it harder and faster and pushed back to meet his thrusts. Kent met her needs by increasing his thrusts until he was moving the couch with each delve into her hot cunt.

Jessie threw back her head and growled as he reached around and fingered her cunt.

"Play with yourself, baby. I can't do it and I want you to come."

She reached between her legs and spread her juices all around her clit as Kent tunneled in and out of her pussy. She rubbed her clit over and over then pressed hard against it and came with a scream.

Her orgasm must have set him off because she felt him go still and taut inside of her as she squeezed his cock. The force of his cum spewing in her cunt sent her off again.

They collapsed against the couch, panting like racehorses after a race.

* * * *

"Wyatt, I know you're there. You can come in." Jessie turned her face to look up at him where he stood on the last step.

"I'm sorry. I was already down before I realized you, um, were..." he trailed off.

"Fucking?" she asked. "It's okay. I liked that you were watching."

"Come on, Jessie. We better get a shower while there's still enough light we can see." Kent stood up and held out his hand to pull her up.

She took his hand and extended her other one to Wyatt for his help as well. What could he do? He grabbed her hand and helped Kent pull her to her feet. He tried not to look at where his brother's seed spilled down the inside of her thigh. He forced his eyes away from the rounded globes of her ass and the gentle swell of her belly. But he got stuck on her breasts. They were beautiful, a little more than a handful, but not a waste at all. Kent caught him staring and grinned.

"She's beautiful, isn't she?"

"Yeah, she is." He let go of Jessie's hand and walked over to the kitchen to get a glass of water.

Somehow, they were going to have to work things out. He couldn't walk in on them like that again. It wasn't right. Jessie was his brother's wife, for want of a better term. It wasn't right for him to see her that way. Hell, it wasn't right that he had jacked off to thoughts of her either.

Then why not join them? It's obvious that you feel something for her. But it wasn't enough. He should love her like she deserved, not just fuck her because she was there and he was horny.

Wyatt cursed and emptied the glass in the sink before leaving it to wash in the morning. He straightened the covers, trying to shut out the obvious scent of sex in the room. Then he climbed into bed and lay awake, waiting for them to come to bed. He didn't want to imagine them in the shower together. He knew what he would do if he had her in the shower. He'd go down on that hot little pussy.

He squeezed his eyes shut and called himself every name in the book. He was not going to think about Jessie that way. She belonged to his brother. They were not going to use her between them like that. End of story.

He heard her shout yes from the bathroom above.

Chapter Nine

"Do you think we're going to get this son of a bitch running again?" Kent asked, dripping sweat from his forehead to the dirty piece of machinery they were working on.

"If it's the last thing I do, I'm going to get the fucker to run." Wyatt cursed when he hit his knuckle on the motor of the tractor.

"Let me look at that book again," Kent said, and wiped his hands with a rag before picking up the book they'd dragged out on motors.

He read back over the last couple of pages and grinned.

"I've got it. It needs more oxygen to generate the spark. There has to be an air filter on it like there is on a car. Let's find it."

They searched and finally found it. The filter came out full of dirt. Kent shook it out and winced when it fell apart in his hand.

"Great, do you think there's another one around here?" Wyatt asked.

"In all this crap? There sure as hell should be." Kent walked over to the wall that had dozens of parts to unknown things hanging or sitting on shelves.

"How are you two getting along?" Wyatt asked as they searched for a filter.

"Fine. Why?"

"Just wanting to be sure I wasn't getting in the way."

"You're my brother. You're never in the way, Wyatt."

"Still, newlyweds need alone time, and we live with each other, so it has to be tough."

"If we need alone time, we can go in one of the other rooms. She's about got them all cleaned up now. Don't worry about it."

"Hmm, what about this?" Wyatt held up a package with a square-shaped thing that looked like a sponge in it.

"Hey, I think that's it. Let's try it. Don't demolish the package. We might need to find more of them."

They carefully pulled it out of the package and placed it in the slot before screwing it back in place. Then they tried to crank the motor again. It took three tries, but it finally took. They popped each other on the arm and crowed in triumph.

"Hey! You got it going!" Jessie handed each of them a glass of tea.

"This is better than yesterday's. I think you got the amount of tea in the thing right this time, baby." Kent took another swallow of the amber liquid.

"Okay, let's start tilling up that garden." Wyatt handed his empty glass back to Jessie. "Thanks, that was good."

She smiled at him then turned and kissed Kent on the lips before grabbing his empty glass and heading back toward the house.

"You can't take your eyes off of her when she's around, Wyatt. I don't care what you say. You love her more than just as a brother. You're hooked on her."

"I said to give it a rest."

Kent shook his head but didn't say anything more. He figured he'd eventually wear him down. It would take time, but what the hell else did they have?

He followed Wyatt out as he drove the tractor with the tines on back. They had staked off the area they wanted to start with for the garden. It wasn't huge, but it was large enough, they figured, to take care of them for the first winter. They were going by one of the books Jessie was always quoting. When she wasn't working, she was reading them.

Wyatt dropped the lever that dug the tines into the ground and shoved the tractor into gear. It ground forward at a snail's pace but dug up the earth as it went. Kent was amazed they were actually getting it to work. Thank God Jessie had insisted they grab those books.

An hour later, Wyatt switched out with him and he drove the tractor, going over and over the same parcel of land until it was a deep, rich bed ready for rowing. His brother was working on the fence line for the small pasture they planned to use for the cow and her calf. He was all for getting them out into the pasture as much as possible. Cleaning cow crap out of the stalls wasn't his favorite thing to do.

By the time it was getting dark, he'd managed to plow up the garden, with half of it ready to row up. By tomorrow, they should have it ready for Jessie to plant. She'd drawn out a map of how she was going to plant, using the book's suggestions on what needed to go next to what. If it could work, she'd get it going.

After they'd all showered and had eaten, they sat around in the dining area of the kitchen at the table and discussed the day's work. It always felt like family time to him. He squeezed Jessie's hand under the table. They tried not to rub Wyatt's nose in it, but he loved touching her.

"So, how far are you on the fence line?" Kent asked.

"About halfway if the rest of the fence is in about the same condition. If it's worse, then it will be a couple more days."

"How are you coming on milking the cow?" Wyatt asked Jessie with a grin.

"Oh, shut up. I'm practicing. It's not easy." She hadn't been able to get more than a glassful of milk so far.

Kent laughed and pinched her ass. She yelped and jumped up to run behind Wyatt.

"Tell him to quit pinching me."

"Kent, you're leaving bruises on her. Stop it."

"I'm not hurting her."

"Kent, stop it." Wyatt grabbed Jessie and hauled her into his lap. "Look at that. You're bruising her." He pointed out a bruise on her hip near her panty line. His hand was cupping her ass.

"Sorry, baby. I didn't know I'd done that." Kent knew he hadn't done it. She'd probably done it walking into something in the dark, like they all did.

What had him, though, was that his brother was unconsciously caressing Jessie's ass. Jessie looked him in the eyes and smiled. It was a start. As if realizing what he was doing, Wyatt suddenly stood up, nearly dropping Jessie in the process.

"I'm going to bed. I'll talk to you in the morning." He walked out of the kitchen and stomped up the stairs.

"I still think my idea is a good one," Jessie said.

"It could backfire on us though, baby." Kent wasn't sure if seducing Wyatt was a good idea or not.

"Once he realizes he enjoys sex with me, the rest will come. I can't help but think he's fighting it anyway. He tries too hard to not be alone with me. He knows you aren't jealous, so why make the effort unless he's fighting the attraction?"

"Give it some more time, baby. If he doesn't give in, in another few weeks, we'll try it your way."

Kent hoped they could convince him soon, because Jessie loved him, and it was killing a part of her knowing he didn't believe he loved her. Maybe a little part of her was afraid he really didn't, and she was only dreaming she saw it in his eyes. Kent wasn't sure what to think, but knew that whatever it took to keep her happy, he would do. That included letting her seduce his brother.

* * * *

Jessie stood up and stretched. Her back was killing her. She'd been planting seeds for the last two hours and felt as if she would never stand up straight again. She looked down the rows of dirt and smiled. All in all, it had been a good day's work. She still had to water it all, but it was in the ground.

She gathered the remainder of the seeds and added them in the basket she would store in the cellar to keep them dry and cool. She didn't have much left. They would have to barter for more next time. Plus, she wanted to get a few different varieties as well. She was learning so much from the books.

"What are you grinning about?" Wyatt asked as he walked up to her.

"I've finished planting everything, and now I'm going to water. It feels good."

"I just finished the pasture for the cow and her calf. They can go out in it tomorrow during the day, and we'll put them up at night. It will give them more to eat and put less work on us."

"Good for you." She hugged him and pulled his head down for a quick kiss.

For once, he didn't immediately pull away or walk off afterwards. She hurried on to keep him from doing it now.

"I'm going to try the water hose we found, but I think it's mostly dry-rotted."

"I'll help you carry water if you need me to."

"Naw, you have things to do. It's not going to hurt me to cart water. I'm strong." She showed him her puny muscles, making him laugh.

"Hey, you two, what's so funny?" Kent walked up with dirt all over him.

"You are. What have you been doing? Playing in the dirt with your toy soldiers?" she asked.

"Funny. I'm cleaning up the shop so we can find what we need out there. It's a mess."

"Is that that building over there that you had the tractor in?"

"Yeah, that's what we are calling it." Kent grinned at her.

She couldn't help but laugh at the cobwebs hanging off his head. She wasn't showering with him tonight.

"You have some room to laugh, Jessie," Wyatt said with a grin. "You're covered in dirt yourself."

"Yeah, but mine is clean dirt. His is old dirt."

Wyatt shook his head and popped her on the ass before walking back toward the house. Jessie smiled at Kent.

"He's coming around. Just wait. I actually kissed him a little while ago, and he didn't run away this time."

"While you two were playing smoochy face, I was working. Not fair." Kent grabbed her around the waist and hauled her up for a kiss.

Jessie moaned when his tongue licked at the seam of her lips. She opened to him and welcomed his tongue into her mouth. He ate at her as if they hadn't just kissed only hours earlier. He devoured her as if they hadn't made love that morning while Wyatt slept.

"Umm, I want you so bad my cock is poking a hole in my jeans."

"Hmm, poor cock."

"Don't you feel sorry for it?"

"Help me unroll this hose over here and I'll check out your hose." Jessie pointed at the rat's nest of garden hose she'd dragged out of the barn earlier.

"That looks like a dirty job."

"I'll clean you up afterwards."

They laughed and began sorting through the garden hoses. Thirty minutes later, she had them stretched out with one end in the garden and the other end hooked to the spigot.

"Ready?" Kent asked.

"Ready."

She watched Kent turn on the water and the hose fill out as water coursed through it. Dozens of tiny pinholes sprayed water everywhere, but the majority of it ran out the other end of the hose into the garden. She whooped for joy.

"So, I helped you. Are you going to help me?"

Jessie laughed and went to her knees. She unfastened his pants so that his thick dick jumped out at her. She licked her lips and looked up at Kent from her position on the ground. He grinned down at her with heavy eyelids.

She wrapped her hand around the base of his cock and licked a long line from top to base and then licked back up again. He hummed in the back of his throat. A drop of pre-cum pearled at the slit, and she licked it off, savoring the taste of him before licking down into the slit for more. Kent hissed and grabbed her head.

"Suck my cock, Jess. Take it all."

She wrapped her lips around him and swallowed down until he reached the back of her throat. Then she swallowed hard around him and backed off. She did it over and over again until he was holding her head still and fucking her mouth with his dick. God, she loved sucking cock. She wanted to taste Wyatt's so badly she ached inside.

She pumped her hand up and down with her mouth until he began groaning. She knew he was close and reached inside his jeans to fondle his balls. He growled and shouted as he shot thick streams of cum down her throat. She swallowed every bit of it and then licked him clean. He pulled away from her and fastened his jeans before helping her to her feet.

"God, you are so damn good at that." He kissed her and wrapped his arms around her before letting her go. "I'd better get back to my job before Wyatt cuts my food supply off for screwing around."

"Ha-ha." Jessie laughed and ran out to the garden to direct the water where she wanted it. She couldn't wait to see her garden grow.

* * * *

Wyatt watched Jessie give Kent a blow job and couldn't help pulling his own cock out of his jeans and tugging on it while he did. He could see just fine from the kitchen window. They were next to the house by the water spigot. He wrapped his fist around his cock and pumped it as he watched Jessie swallow Kent's down her throat.

By the time Kent was face fucking her, Wyatt was about ready to come. He wanted to make it last as long as Kent lasted, but he was too fucking horny. He'd been hard ever since he'd woken up to them fucking next to him. He'd pretended not to be awake, but knowing they were having sex in bed with him had grown his cock and left it that way all day long.

He squeezed his balls and locked his knees as he felt the first electrical shocks in his spine signaling his imminent release. He squeezed hard on his cock and caught the streams of cum in his hand. He wanted to shout out but didn't want them to know what he was doing. It felt so wrong to be jerking off watching them have oral sex.

Wyatt groaned at the sight of Jessie licking all the cum from his brother's dick. He looked down where he was cupping his cum and about to dispose of it. What he wouldn't have given to have had her swallow his cum. What was wrong with him? Why couldn't he get her out of his head? She belonged to his brother and deserved to be loved for her and not for her body. All he could give her would be his body, because he couldn't love her, too, could he?

He hurriedly cleaned up and fixed a glass of tea as Jessie finished fiddling with the water hose and headed for the house. She walked inside as he took his first sip of tea.

"Oh, man. Just what I need. She took the glass away from him and swallowed down half the glass.

"Help yourself, Jessie," he said with a grin.

She smiled and winked at him, then filled it back up and handed it to him. "Thanks."

"Looks like you got the water hose to work—for the most part."

"Yeah, Kent helped me unravel it and hook it up. I think it will work. The next time we go raid a place, let's look for garden hoses, though."

"I was thinking about that. Maybe in another week we should look at that town called Skyline on the map. There's bound to be a few stores there we can look through."

Jessie grinned and jumped up and down like a kid. "Oh boy! Shopping." She reached up and dragged him down for a kiss.

He forgot himself and kissed her back. She latched on to his tongue and sucked it in, teasing it with her own. He moaned and wrapped his arms around her as she shoved her tongue into his mouth. He slid his along hers and then realized what he was doing. When he tried to peel her arms from around his neck, she whimpered and held on. He gripped her waist and tried pulling her off of him, but she wouldn't let go.

When she finally came up for air, she was panting and whimpering.

"Please don't push me away, Wyatt. Please don't."

"Jess, you don't understand. It's not right."

"It is right. I love you, and I know you love me, whether you believe it or not."

Wyatt ran a hand through his shaggy hair and tried to think of what he could say to make her understand.

"Jessie. There was someone in college that I fell in love with."

She stilled and stepped back.

"I don't know what I feel for you, Jessie. I can't promise it's what you need. What you deserve."

"You love someone else? All this time, and you've never said anything. Does Kent even know about her?"

"No. My parents didn't even know about her, and then they were all gone."

"Why are you telling me?"

"Because I don't want to hurt you, and I'm afraid that I will in the end. I'm afraid that all I'll be doing is using you, and that isn't right."

Jessie swallowed hard. He watched her throat convulse as she seemed to be fighting something.

"I'm sorry, Wyatt. I didn't know. I won't force myself on you anymore." She took a step back and then another and bumped into the kitchen table.

Then she turned around and walked through the living room. He heard her footsteps on the stairs, and he realized he might have just done what he'd sworn he never would. He had hurt her.

Chapter Ten

Kent walked inside an hour before dark and headed straight for the shower. He was a nasty mess and needed to clean up before he helped with anything inside. He hadn't seen anyone when he walked in and was a little surprised to see Jessie lying on the bed in the bedroom when he got upstairs.

He quietly walked over to the bed and bent over to see if she was asleep. Her eyes were closed. She looked tired. Maybe she'd come in early for a nap. He decided not to wake her. He'd take a shower instead. She'd wake up when he got out to dry off and dress.

He scrubbed all the cobwebs, dirt, and gunk from his body. Then he worked on getting it from beneath his nails, the best he could. He couldn't help but think about the blow job he'd gotten earlier. She'd surprised him with that. He really hadn't expected her to go down on him right outside in the middle of the yard like that, but it had been fucking hot.

When he got out of the shower and dried off, he walked in to find that Jessie was gone. *Hmm, she must have gone downstairs to start supper, then.* He finished dressing in clean jeans but left the shirt off. It was too hot for a shirt, anyway.

He found her in the kitchen stirring noodles on the stove. She'd opened a can of tomatoes and was going to make a pasta dish of some sort, it looked like. Just as he started to lay his lips on the back of her neck, Wyatt walked in from outside. She turned around and nearly screamed at him standing over her.

"Fuck! You scared me to death, Kent." She sat the spoon down on the spoon rest on the stove and wiped her hands on the apron she had on.

"Sorry. I didn't mean to. He kissed her on the lips then moved back out of the way.

He could tell something was wrong, but he didn't know what it was. He sighed and decided to leave it alone until after supper. Only after supper, they talked about the garden and what to work on next, and then she wanted to go to bed early.

"I'm really tired. My back is hurting some. I'm obviously not in shape for this kind of work." She laughed.

"Rest up, baby. I'll be up soon."

"Night, Wyatt."

She didn't hug him like she normally did. Her back must really have been hurting, he decided. He would offer a backrub if she was still awake when he got upstairs.

"The garden looks really good. She's worked hard on it," Wyatt said.

"Yeah. She's managed to do a lot in the two weeks we've been here. I'm surprised she's held up this long. She needs a day off, I think."

"Good idea. Why don't you two stay inside all day tomorrow and just relax. I'm going to work around the outside of the house some and make a list of things we might need. I told her we might think about hitting that city on the map called Skyline. She wants new garden hoses, for one thing."

"Sounds good. I'll keep her inside tomorrow and get her to rest some. When do you want to head to the city?" Kent asked.

"I was thinking about a couple of days. I want to make sure I have a good list of things. You should be thinking about what you know we need, too. We can all three combine our lists and figure out where to go once we get there."

Kent stretched. "I think I'm going on up. Don't stay up too late if you're going to be handling the work tomorrow."

"I'll be up in a few minutes," Wyatt said.

Kent climbed the stairs and found Jessie still awake in bed. She looked worn out, and maybe even a little sad.

"Hey, baby. How about a back rub?"

"Oh, you don't have to do that. I'll be fine in the morning."

"I want to. I like rubbing my hands all over your bare skin."

"I'm wearing a T-shirt, silly." She rolled over anyway and gave him her back.

"Yeah, but I can run my hands up under that nasty T-shirt of yours and touch to my heart's content."

He did so and began a slow, gentle massage up and down her spine until he felt her slowly release and relax.

"Better?"

"Yeah." She rolled back over, and when he lay down, she rolled back on top of him to lay her head on his chest. "Kent?"

"Yeah, baby?"

"I think I'm going to leave Wyatt alone now. I'm making him uncomfortable, and I'm not getting anywhere. If he changes his mind, then we can think about it."

"Something happen, Jess?" Kent stilled.

"No. I've just been thinking about it and realized that it's not fair to push on him and tease him if he doesn't want to be involved. I can't make him."

"Whatever you want to do, Jessie. I'll support you."

Kent felt a piece of him tear away as he realized he wouldn't have his brother's help in loving his Jessie. Sure, he knew that if anything happened to him that Wyatt would always take care of her. But it wouldn't be the same. Part of him understood why she was giving up, and part of him didn't. If she loved him as much as she said she did, why give up at all?

"I love you, Kent." She squeezed him and settled her head over his heart.

"I love you, too." He wrapped his arms around her and held her close.

About thirty minutes later, Jessie was asleep in his arms, and Wyatt came to bed. Neither man felt comfortable that someone wouldn't steal Jessie from them, so they continued to share the king-size bed. Kent began to wonder if he would still do that in the future.

Wyatt always slept in his underwear, but tonight, he slept in his jeans as well. Something had happened. He just didn't know what, and he wasn't going to ask either one of them. As much as he wanted to know, he didn't want to stir up the pain that both of them were obviously feeling. The piece of him that had torn away grew bigger, and he knew that as long as the three of them were at odds, it would never get better.

* * * *

"How much longer, Kent?" Jessie asked as they drove toward Skyline.

"Looks like another thirty minutes, maybe."

"Wyatt, what happens if we can't find gas to get back?"

"We'll find gas or siphon it out of cars there. Stop worrying."

They'd left at the crack of dawn to head for Skyline in hopes of finding some of the things on their wish list. Jessie had a long list, but the top four things were all she was really worried about. She wanted canning supplies, garden hoses, cheesecloth, and more matches. The cheesecloth was to skim the milk she was finally growing better at getting, and the matches were for emergencies. The pilot lights had all blown out after a big windy storm they'd had one night. Evidently the house wasn't as airtight as they'd first assumed. She wanted to be sure they had plenty. Kent had added beside it flint in case they ran out of matches. She wasn't sure where they would find that, but she had it down.

Sitting between the two men was eating at her. She scooted a little closer to Kent. Touching Wyatt only made her ache inside, and she knew she had no chance there anymore. He had treated her just like a sister-in-law after that afternoon, and she reciprocated. It had been hard the last few days, but it was for the best.

"Look, I think those are the suburbs of the city." Kent pointed out some houses that were in neat rows.

"It's so spooky looking, knowing no one lives here anymore."

"Not any different than the places we passed through on our way across country," Wyatt pointed out.

"I guess it's because we've been living on our own for a while. Now we are going to town, and you expect there to be people." Jessie watched the houses pass.

They drove around for a little while then found a gas station that seemed to have electricity. Wyatt got out and checked the area but found no one. He filled the truck up with gas and they moved on.

"There's a sporting goods store, Wyatt," Kent pointed out.

His brother grunted and pulled into the parking lot. There was no sign of wolves, but Kent and Wyatt warned her to stay inside the truck until they checked it out. They climbed out and carried guns inside the building. When they returned, she climbed out of the truck and walked slowly with them back inside.

"Someone has already been here. All the guns and ammunition are gone, and someone has been through the clothes," Kent told her.

"Well, let's just see what we can find on our lists and move on."

She found two pair of boots in her size and a couple of sets of thermals that would fit her. She grabbed several coats that would fit and then went in search of the matches and flint. She found both and loaded them into the bucket she'd also found.

"Here, baby. Let me carry that out to the truck for you." Kent grabbed her stuff and walked out to the truck to load it with some things Wyatt was already loading up.

She found several magazines on preparing wild meats and added them to a pile of stuff by the front door. A noise in the back of the store startled her. She froze and listened again. Maybe it had been her imagination. Nothing more moved. She walked behind the counter, searching for anything more that might be of use.

By the time the men had finished loading the truck, she'd thought of something. She wasn't sure what they would think about it, but it was smart to her. They needed to get a truck from one of the car dealerships for trips when they only wanted a few things, and it wouldn't burn so much gas. Plus, they could use it around the farm. They would be spreading out some as they lived there. She would spring it on them once they were on their way again.

As she walked toward the front door to see how the men were coming, something knocked her down from behind. She screamed and covered her head with her hands expecting any minute for something to bite her. Instead, she felt a tongue lapping at her hands.

"What in the hell?"

"What is it?" Kent's voice sounded confused.

Jessie just wanted them to get whatever it was off of her. She screamed at them to get it off.

"Whoa, there, baby. It's a dog of some sort." Kent pulled her to her feet and was immediately assaulted again by a horse of a dog.

"Where in the hell did it come from?" Wyatt asked.

"I don't know. It just attacked me from behind."

"It must have been in the back of the store somewhere and we just didn't see it."

"How could you have missed something this big?" she wanted to know.

"What do we do with it?" Kent asked.

"Wyatt, we can't leave it here."

"It's too big to ride up front with us, and I don't think it would survive in the back of the truck all that way."

"I think we need to get a truck from one of the car dealerships, anyway. It can ride in the back of the bed." She filled them in on what she thought about getting a truck to use around the farm.

"What do you think?" Wyatt asked Kent.

"Sounds like a good idea to me. We can get one on the way out of town and gas it up. For now, the dog will do okay in the back of the truck for the short rides we are taking," Kent said.

Jessie eyed the massive hound and shook her head. He would be a mess to deal with, but since they had wolves around, it wouldn't be a bad idea to have something around to help guard the house. He was sort of cute, in an ugly kind of way.

They loaded up and headed to another store. This time, they found a Kmart near a car dealership and pulled around behind it to the loading docks. When they opened the back of the truck, the dog bounded out and up to the door as if knowing they would be going inside.

"You know, he's too young for someone to have owned him before all hell broke loose. Why is he so damn well behaved and not wild?" Kent pointed out.

"I don't know. Do you think there's someone who lives around here, and we're taking their dog?" Jessie asked.

"Naw."

Wyatt finally got the door opened, and they all filed inside with the dog running off ahead of them.

"I guess if there are any wolves in here, he'll flush them out," Wyatt said.

"That's not a warm and fuzzy thought," she complained.

When nothing growled, howled, or attacked, they split up with their lists and carts and agreed to meet back in an hour. Jessie loaded her cart with all the canning supplies she could find then piled on some other things from her lists. She parked her cart at the back of the store and grabbed another. She searched the grocery aisles for cheesecloth and finally found it hanging on one of the canned good aisles. She took it all.

Then she raced to finish her lists and meet the men back at the back with her second cart. She noticed the dog was sitting there as if waiting on them. She shook her head. Then Wyatt showed up with a cart piled high with mechanical stuff. Kent wasn't far behind him with what appeared to be even more mechanical stuff.

"Don't you guys have enough of that stuff to play with out in your shop?"

"Nope," they both said in union.

"Well, since you didn't get any clothes, I'm going to have to go back and shop some more. You can go ahead and load all this up while I grab winter gear for you two numskulls.

"Great idea," Kent said, and ducked when she threw a roll of paper towels at him.

Growling, she grabbed an empty cart and went in search of men's winter wear. The dog followed her around as she added to the cart.

"They can be such babies sometimes. I have to follow behind them, and pick up after them, and remind them to wipe their feet." She looked over at the dog. "Why am I talking to you, anyway?"

The dog whined.

"Jessie?" Kent's voice called through the store.

"I'm over in the sporting goods," she called back.

"What are you doing over here?" he asked when he walked up.

"Looking for hats, gloves, and scarves for you guys."

"You about ready to go?"

"Whenever you are. I could grab stuff all day, though."

"We'll be back in a couple of months before the snows hit. Let's go find a truck. You can pick out the color, but Wyatt and I are picking out the rest."

"Come on, Dog. We're going truck hunting. You can take point." She laughed at the expression on Kent's face.

In the end, they drove home a shiny new Dodge Ram pickup in a midnight-black color. It got good gas mileage for a truck and had everything in it the men wanted. It even had a DVD player, and they'd gone back to Kmart just to get DVDs to watch on Saturday nights. They would have to watch them in the truck, but the men thought that was fine. She truly felt that the men had lost their minds.

She and Kent drove it to the house while Wyatt drove the U-Haul. They made it back home about five that night and spent the next few hours unloading the truck.

They let the cow and her calf out for a few hours to get some exercise until they finished everything. The dog ran around the farm but was back under their feet after every circle he made.

Jessie watched the men go bring in the cow and calf, but all of them stood back as the dog herded the animals up to the gate, where Wyatt slipped the rope around the cow's neck and led her to the barn. The calf followed along, but even if it hadn't, the dog would have nosed it along.

"I think we have a cow dog," Wyatt said.

"Well, he needs a name," she said.

"What's wrong with Dog?" Kent asked.

"Kent." Jessie popped him on the arm.

"Well, we'll think of a name soon enough," Wyatt said. "Let's lock up the trucks and get something to eat before bed. I'm exhausted."

Jessie laughed and headed for the house. She walked inside and screamed.

Chapter Eleven

Kent and Wyatt ran for the house but didn't see Jessie anywhere. They could hear the dog inside the house growling and barking wildly. Kent opened the door and the dog bounded out and around the side of the house. They heard horses' hooves around the front of the house as the dog barked and growled.

The men rounded the house in time to see someone on a horse carrying Jessie over their saddle and riding off through the woods. The dog ran after them, close on their heels.

"Fuck! He has her, Wyatt. How in the hell are we going to get her back?" Kent's voice shook with rage.

The dog ran back and then returned to the woods as if begging them to follow him.

"The dog can lead us to her. Come on." Kent started to follow the dog, but Wyatt stopped him.

"We need the guns. Hold up, Dog. We're coming." The dog whined but waited on them.

They each grabbed guns and set out after the dog in hopes of finding Jessie unharmed. They knew she would have fought like hell and to be lying over the horse, she had to have been unconscious. Kent was about to lose his mind and could tell Wyatt was just as crazy. They had never thought anyone would be in the house waiting on them. Hell, they hadn't thought of anyone coming out there to take Jessie at all in the last few weeks. They'd become complacent in their belief that they were the only ones in the world out there.

"Wyatt, I can't live without her."

"We'll get her back, brother. We'll get her back."

They followed the dog and the obvious trail for over an hour before the dog began to walk around in circles. He whined and started one way, only to go another. Kent studied the ground and finally figured out what had happened. For some reason, the horse had thrown them. The horse went one way, and the man went another. By the depth of the tracks, he was carrying Jessie. This would slow him down.

They followed the footprints, which had the dog on track again. Dog barked and growled periodically but continued to trail Jessie and her captor. Kent and Wyatt called out for Jessie over and over but got no answer. If she were able to, she would be screaming her head off. They were beginning to worry that they might have lost them when they came upon a house. It was almost full dark now. The house was obviously lived in and had electricity by the lights inside.

"Do you think they have her here?" Kent asked, bringing the rifle up.

"I don't know, Kent. We'll find out. Dog will know if she's here."

They headed up to the back of the house around the garden. Dog wasn't happy about changing course. They had to encourage him to follow them, and he kept going back to the woods.

"I don't think she's here," Kent said.

"Hold it right there," a deep voice said behind them in the dark.

Kent and Wyatt stilled.

"Drop your guns and step away from them."

"We don't mean any harm. We're looking for our woman," Wyatt said.

"With guns?"

"Someone stole her from the house, and we're following them." Kent strained to see the man behind the voice, but the night kept him hidden.

"Brandon?" A woman's voice called out from the direction of the house.

"Stay inside, Heather. Where's Bolton?"

"I've got her." Another male voice sounded behind where the female voice had come from.

"You understand how we feel if you have a woman. We're just trying to find her before he hurts her," Wyatt said in a tight voice.

"Who has her?" the first voice asked.

"We don't know. She went in the house, and we heard a scream. Then a horse and rider rode by with her. About a mile back, the horse must have thrown them, because he's on foot now."

"Bolton, stay here with Heather. I'm going to help these guys. I'll be back."

"Be careful, Brandon," the female named Heather called out.

"Come on. They're on my land now. I'll show you how to find them. My name's Brandon."

"I'm Wyatt, and this is my brother Kent." Wyatt held out his hand and they shook.

"Let's get your woman back."

Kent and Wyatt followed Brandon through the woods with dog leading the way. After a few minutes of following the dog, the man stopped.

"He's heading for the west road. He probably has a truck parked there and plans to reach it. We'll get there faster if we go back and take my truck, but you have to trust me on this."

Kent looked at Wyatt to see what he thought. Together, they nodded at Brandon. They'd trust him. They ran back to the house and jumped in Brandon's truck. Dog and Kent got in the back while Wyatt climbed up front with Brandon. The man pulled out of the drive like a bat out of hell.

They made it to the road just as a man emerged with Jessie over his shoulder. He saw them and threw her in the back of the truck before jumping in the front. Brandon pulled up beside him just as he pulled out and slammed into the side of the other truck, knocking it back to the side of the road.

Kent jumped over into the truck bed and grabbed for Jessie, cradling her head in his lap to keep her from banging around on the truck. She had a nasty gash on her head and a busted lip. The bastard had hit her. He would kill him for that alone.

Kent risked a glance over at Brandon's truck and saw that they were swerving over to hit them again. He braced himself and held Jessie tight in his arms. When the other man managed to outmaneuver them, he got up and rested Jessie's head against his side. He reached through the rear window where it was open and grabbed the man by the head, trying to keep him from being able to drive.

His plan worked in that the man lost control of the truck, but it backfired when they hit a tree. He ended up halfway through the back window and was scared to death of where Jessie had landed. He pulled himself back through and found her crumpled next to the cab. She was moaning. God, had he made it worse by losing his temper?

"Jessie, baby." Wyatt was suddenly there in the back of the truck, holding her. "Baby, please say something."

"Kent, make her say something."

Wyatt was about out of it, he was so upset. Kent wrapped his arm around his brother and his woman and felt the tears falling as they rocked her together.

"Let me have a look at her. I've had some first aid. Let me see. I'll be careful with her. I promise." Brandon carefully eased between them. They let him.

Kent watched as the stranger checked Jessie over. Wyatt's face was covered in tears, and he wouldn't let go of her hand. The other man backed off then.

"She's got a concussion, but I don't feel anything broken. It'll all depend on how bad the head injury is. Let's get her back to my house. My wife can sew her head up, and we'll take care of her."

"Where's the bastard that did this to her?" Wyatt stood up to jump out of the truck.

"He's dead. Broken neck. Wasn't wearing his seat belt," the other man said.

"Good riddance." Kent picked Jessie up and eased to the end of the truck.

Wyatt lowered the tailgate and took Jessie from Kent while he jumped down.

"Sorry about your truck, Brandon," Wyatt said as he brushed the hair from Jessie's face.

"Don't worry about it. I'll get another one when I go to Skyline."

Dog kept nosing at Wyatt's hands where he held Jessie. Kent rubbed the dog's head, then opened the front cab door to climb in the truck so he could take Jessie from Wyatt. His brother hesitated in letting her go. He knew how he felt. He didn't want her out of his sight now, either.

They drove slowly back to the house. When they arrived the front door opened and Bolton and Heather walked out to greet them.

"Is she okay?" Heather asked.

"She's going to need stitches. She has a head injury." Brandon wrapped his arm around the woman.

"Come on in and we'll take care of her for you." Bolton stood to the side of the door and held it open.

* * * *

Jessie hurt all over but was afraid to open her eyes. She didn't know where she was, but it wasn't at home. The bed felt different, and the house smelled different. She heard a noise next to her and nearly jumped when someone touched her. She couldn't stop the groan when she moved her head.

"Easy, baby. Don't move."

That was Wyatt's voice. She opened her eyes and looked around without moving her head. She wasn't at home, but it was Wyatt holding her hand with tears in his eyes.

"Wyatt?"

"Hey, baby. I've been so worried. Kent and I've been taking turns seeing about you for the last few days."

"Days? Where am I?"

"You're at Brandon, Bolton, and Heather's house. They live a few miles from our place. We met them when we were looking for you. They helped us get you back, and then helped take care of you because you were hurt."

"What's wrong with me?"

"You had a head injury, baby. We think the horse threw you, and then with the truck hitting the tree, you hit it again. We've been worried sick."

Jessie closed her eyes then opened them again. "You said for days. How many days have I been unconscious?"

"Three."

"Kent's okay?"

"He's fine. He was here earlier. We keep trading out to take care of the farm and see about you."

"I'm sorry I've been so much trouble." Jessie felt the tears falling even before they fell.

Wyatt had a cloth at her eyes as they rolled down her cheeks.

"Don't cry, baby. It's all going to be fine." Wyatt caressed her cheek. "I thought I'd lost you."

"Oh, Wyatt. I'm going to be okay. I just have a headache."

"I love you, Jessie. I honestly do. Can you ever forgive me for doubting my feelings?"

Jessie looked at him, unable to believe what she'd heard. "You said you love me?"

"I did, I do. I love you with all my heart. When I realized I might lose you, I thought my life was over with. There's nothing without you, baby."

"I love you, Wyatt. I never stopped loving you."

"I'm sorry I hurt you, Jess. I never meant to, but I thought what I was feeling was wrong. I thought I was doing the right thing by stepping back for Kent."

"It's okay. Everything is going to be okay now." She palmed his cheek with her hand and blew a kiss at him.

Wyatt leaned over and gently brushed her lips with his. "You rest now. I'm going to let Heather know you're awake, so she can introduce herself and check on you."

"I love you."

Jessie watched him leave, and a few minutes later, a small woman of about twenty-two walked in carrying a bowl and a glass. She had long red hair pulled back in a braid and the prettiest blue eyes.

"I'm Heather, your next-door neighbor." She sat the bowl and glass on the table by the bed. "Let's check your head."

Jessie waited as she fiddled with the bandage on her head and then refastened it.

"It looks good. You'll have a scar. I'm sorry, but I'm not a doctor."

"That's okay, I appreciate that you helped me. How long have you lived here?"

"A little over a year now." She held the bowl up and spooned a little of the broth into Jessie's mouth for her.

"Mmm, that's good."

"It's deer stew. You're just getting the broth from it, though. You can't have anything solid till tomorrow. You've been unconscious for three days. We were getting worried."

"I don't think I can eat much. My head really hurts." Jessie closed her eyes, willing her headache to go away.

"I'll get you something for your head then. Hold on." Heather got up and walked out but returned a few seconds later with something for her to take.

"Rest now. You'll feel better when you wake up."

"I didn't realize you were pregnant." Jessie noticed Heather's slightly protruding belly.

"Yes, we're excited."

"Congratulations."

"Rest now," Heather said.

Jessie closed her eyes to rest but didn't sleep again. She knew the minute that Kent walked into the room. She forced her eyes open and smiled at him. He knelt by the bed and grabbed her hand.

"Jessie, honey. I thought I had lost you." He hiccupped. "Don't ever leave me, baby. I can't make it without you."

"I'm not going anywhere, Kent." She squeezed his hand. "I'm fine. I want to go home."

"Not until Heather thinks it's safe enough for you to travel."

"It's only a few miles."

"It's a bumpy ride, though. I'm not putting you through it until Heather thinks you'll be okay to go. You're safe here. Brandon and Bolton are good men."

"She lives with two men, too?"

"Yep, and believe it or not, they're brothers, as well."

"It will be nice to have a friend close by," Jessie confessed.

"Our lands meet. In fact, it looks like our cow and calf came from their herd."

"Oh, no. I love that calf."

"We get to keep them." Kent laughed. "They made it a housewarming gift."

"Ask Heather when I can go home. I want to be in my own bed."

"I'll ask, baby. You get some more sleep. Wyatt will be here when you wake up again."

"Love you, Kent."

"I love you, Jessie."

Jessie couldn't keep her eyes open, but when Heather poked her head back in later to ask if she wanted something to eat, she jumped at the chance to talk.

"What would you like to talk about?" Heather asked, sitting on the edge of the bed.

"Are Bolton and Brandon both your men? I mean, well, are they your lovers?"

"Yes, they are. They're my husbands. Aren't you with Wyatt and Kent?"

"Sort of." She looked away.

"What do you mean?"

"Kent and I are lovers, but Wyatt has been trying to stay away because he thinks it's wrong to love me when his brother does. But I think maybe he's changed his mind, and I was hoping you were living that way, too. It would go a long way in helping him accept me."

"I don't think you have to worry about Wyatt anymore. He's been beside himself worried about you. Give it some time, though. You've been seriously hurt, and he isn't going to want to take a chance of hurting you more. In fact, neither of your men are going to want to have sex anytime soon, because they are going to be worried about you."

"You sound like you're talking from experience." Jessie tried to rearrange herself in the bed.

"I was attacked by a wolf and got really sick. I basically had to demand my rights before they would touch me that way." She held out her arm to show Jessie the bite marks up and down her arm.

"You were lucky! That had to have hurt so badly." Jessie couldn't imagine living through something like that.

"It wasn't fun, but then I'm sure your head hasn't felt too good, either."

"I really appreciate everything you have done for me and my men, but when can I go home? I want my own bed." Jessie tried not to sound ungrateful.

"I figured you were going to ask that. If you can hold down solid food tomorrow, you can go home tomorrow night."

"Thank you. I really do appreciate everything."

"Hey, I understand. I wouldn't want to be away from my husbands, either. You'll get well and work out your differences, and everything will be fine. Just give them a little time to get over nearly losing you."

"Maybe when I'm better, we can visit some, and you can tell me what I need to know about living through the winter. I'm new to all of this, and I'm afraid I'm not thinking about everything we need."

"I'm no expert, I can assure you of that, but I'll tell you everything that we did and we'll get you winter-ready."

"I think we're going to be good friends, Heather," Jessie said with a smile.

"I'm counting on it."

Chapter Twelve

"How do you feel, baby?" Wyatt asked as he settled her into the bed.

"I'm fine, Wyatt. I'm so glad to be home." Jessie smoothed her hands over the covers.

Kent walked in with a glass of tea and some medicine for her to take. He sat the glass on the bedside table and handed her the pills.

"Heather said you had to take this when you got home." Kent handed her the glass of tea once she'd put the pills in her mouth.

"Kent, I'm going to run and check on the animals and be right back." Wyatt kissed Jessie on the lips and ran out the door.

Kent caught her looking toward the door and chuckled. "He'll be back soon. You saw him run."

"I'm almost afraid to believe, Kent." Jessie searched her lover's eyes for any sign that he was jealous.

"Believe it. He's made it clear to me that he plans on being your husband as well."

"How do you feel about that? I mean, we were fine with it to begin with, but then he stepped back, and we were just us for a while." Jessie was so scared it would all blow up in her face.

"I'm perfectly happy about it. It's what I've wanted all along. I love him, he's my brother. I wouldn't want another man near you, but Wyatt will always be a part of us." Kent bent over and kissed her.

"Did I miss anything?" Wyatt bounded back in the room out of breath.

"Did you really run all the way out there and back?" Jessie asked.

"Yes. I didn't want to miss a minute of being with you."

"Oh, Wyatt. I love you so much." Jessie reached up to grab his hand.

"I love you. I'm going to go take a shower so I can get in bed and hold you." Wyatt bent over and kissed her before heading to the bathroom.

"We've created a monster," Kent said with a smile.

"I think he's sort of cute." Jessie sighed and relaxed against the pillows. "Where is Dog?"

"He's in the barn with the cows. We let him in to see you at Heather's house a few times, and he's been okay since we brought you home. We'll let him in to see you tomorrow. We owe him because he tracked you for us. We would never have made it to Brandon and Bolton's if Dog hadn't led us there."

Kent began undressing. He stripped down to nothing and climbed into bed, pulling her toward him.

"Am I hurting your head?" he asked.

"No, I'm fine. It feels good to be in your arms."

Kent rubbed his hands up and down her arms. It felt so good to be home. She had been so afraid when the man had grabbed her and slung her over his shoulder. She'd frozen. It had been as if all her nightmares had come to life again. When the horse had thrown them, she'd tried to get away, but he'd hit her, and she passed out when she hit her head. She didn't think she would have been able to live without Wyatt and Kent. They were her life.

"Is there room for me?" Wyatt asked from the other side of the bed.

"Plenty of room. Climb in," Jessie said, holding out her hand to him.

Wyatt climbed into the bed totally naked and snuggled up to her on the opposite side of Kent. Jessie rolled over and snuggled her ass up to Kent's cock and wrapped her arm around Wyatt's chest. She kissed him and rested her head on his shoulder. This is what she wanted to do for the rest of her life. Sleep between her men.

* * * *

Jessie was about ready to scream by the time the men let her out of bed to go outside and walk around. Four days at Heather's and then three days in bed at the house had just about driven her crazy. She needed to get some fresh air and finally convinced them to let her. They set up a chair and table with tea so she could watch them work in the garden and around the house.

She had yet to get them to make love to her. She planned to change that tonight. If she didn't make the first move, they might never touch her that way again. She wasn't having any of that.

Wyatt returned to check on her every few minutes. Kent was by almost as regularly. She didn't know how they got any work done. Dog lay at her feet, occasionally licking her as if to assure that she was there. Three men to watch over her. What woman wouldn't be in heaven?

"Look at these peas," Wyatt said, handing her a few string beans. "Are they ready, or do they need a few more days?"

"Give them another day or two to fill out. The tomatoes over there look ripe. Be sure and get them. I'll make spaghetti with some of the noodles that we have."

"You don't need to be on your feet that long, Jessie. We'll cook," Wyatt insisted.

"I'm tired of sitting around. If I don't do something, I'm going to go bonkers and drive you crazy."

"We'll see when you go inside how you feel then."

Jessie growled at him. He just laughed and headed over to the tomatoes with the bucket. She watched him choose the ripe ones and gently place them in the bucket. She had taught him well. He found out he didn't like bruised tomatoes.

Kent walked up and crouched next to her. He absently rubbed Dog's head and leaned in and kissed her. She smiled and grabbed his ears and pulled him in for a proper kiss. He opened his mouth in surprise, and she slipped her tongue inside to slide along his. When he moaned and placed a hand on her cheek, she knew she had him. He'd be much more susceptible to her advances tonight.

They pulled apart reluctantly when Wyatt walked up and cleared his throat.

"Don't you think it's a little soon for that?"

"Nope," they both said together.

Jessie reached out and grabbed his hardened cock through his jeans before he realized what she was about to do. He groaned but didn't immediately pull back as she scraped her nails up and down the length of him.

"Fuck, baby. I'm going to come in my jeans if you don't stop."

"I can't have that. I want that cock inside of me tonight.

"I don't know," Kent began.

"Don't you dare try and say I'm not well enough. If you don't take care of me, I'll take care of myself." Jessie gave them her best pissed-off expression. She could tell it was working.

"Maybe if we're really careful," Wyatt said.

"We can try and see how she does," Kent agreed.

She had them by the balls and knew it. She'd seal the deal when she took a nice, long bath and soaked, wishing for her favorite bath salts. She just had to ask one of the men to heat up a couple of buckets of water for her.

In the end, they heated up three and had a nice warm bath set up for her when she went inside. The salts added a fresh scent in the air. She stepped into the delightfully sudsy water and lowered herself into the tub. It felt like heaven.

"That too warm, baby?" Kent asked, hovering by her.

"Nope, it's just right. Now go on and leave me alone to enjoy my bath."

Kent and Wyatt backed out of the bathroom reluctantly. She smiled and sank below the water until just her head poked up. She wanted to be soft and smell good for them. She'd shave her legs and wash her hair. She hadn't washed it since she'd hit her head, and it had dried blood in it. Kent had taken the stitches out that morning, so she could get it wet now if she were careful.

After completing her bath ritual, she got out of the tub and dried off. She rubbed her hair as dry as she could get it and then ran the comb through it. She applied lotion and slipped into a little nothing of a gown.

She peeked out of the door and saw the men lounging on the bed totally naked. They'd obviously showered in the other bathroom. They only had cold water to bathe in, but now their cocks stood at attention. She opened the door and walked into the bedroom toward her men.

* * * *

Wyatt stared at the vision walking toward them. She was so damn beautiful. He couldn't believe he'd waited all this time to be with her. She was heaven right there on earth and in their home.

"Come here, baby." Kent patted the bed between him and his brother. "Climb right on up here."

Wyatt wasn't sure what to say. All of a sudden he felt tongue-tied.

Jessie climbed sensually in the bed, moving like a cat. She ran her hand up his leg and around his aching cock but didn't touch it. Instead, she raked her nails across his nipples, sending shivers down his spine.

"I want you guys, and I'm not taking no for an answer."

"I don't think we can say no, baby," Kent confessed. He held his arms out to her.

Jessie turned over and lay on her back, putting her hands on both of their cocks, and squeezed them. They each issued a drop of pre-cum. She smoothed it over their dicks and rubbed them up and down.

Wyatt groaned and reached for her hand to still her. "I'm going to come, and I'm not ready to yet."

"I want someone to suck my nipples and someone to suck my pussy." Jessie continued to play with them.

"I call pussy," Kent said.

"I've got those pretty tits covered." Wyatt rolled over and began unlacing her nightgown.

It took him a few seconds to finally get it off of her. Below, Kent was removing her thong with his teeth.

Wyatt licked each nipple, enjoying how they instantly pebbled for him. He loved her nipples and how hard they got for him. He molded her breasts, then latched on to one of her nipples and sucked. God, he couldn't get enough of them. He forced all of her breast he could get into his mouth and then backed off to treat the other one to the same attention. When he let go this time, he began to pinch and twist them, knowing she liked it by the little whimpers she was making and the fact that she thrust them closer to his hands.

Below, he noticed Kent giving her long, slow licks before plunging his tongue deep inside of her. She bucked beneath them when he dipped a finger within her hot cunt. Wyatt grinned. His brother would find her hot spot and have her moaning and whimpering louder before long.

He nipped at her tit then nibbled all around her nipple with his teeth. When he licked over them, she grabbed his face and buried his mouth on them.

"Suck them hard, Wyatt. I'm going to come. I want you both eating me when I do." She was breathless as she made her demands, then threw back her head to scream.

Wyatt latched on to one and sucked it hard and deep into his mouth while twisting and pinching the other one. When she gasped and screamed again, he knew she was coming. He redoubled his effort, wanting it to be good for her.

As she finally gave out, he stopped and licked both nipples with long, slow swipes of his tongue. Then he pulled her into his arms and kissed her. He felt Kent climb up on the other side of her and spoon her from behind.

"We're not finished, boys. I want you to fuck me, and I want one of you in my mouth. I just need a breather."

"Baby, you're not rested enough for that. We just wanted to please you and take the edge off of you first."

Wyatt crawled to the end of the bed after a few minutes and stretched her sweet pussy with two fingers. He wanted to make sure she would be ready for him. Then he lined his aching dick up with her dripping cunt and plunged in.

She screamed out, "Yes!"

"Baby, open up that pretty mouth. I want my cock between your lips." Kent held his cock poised by her face.

When she opened her mouth it wasn't to take him in, but to lick him. She ran her tongue up and down his dick as Wyatt watched. His cock grew even harder, if that was possible, at the sight of their woman pleasuring his brother.

Her pussy was heaven itself, all hot and tight and wet. He pulled out, then pushed back in. Over and over he tunneled in and out of her hot depths. He wanted to pound into her but wasn't going to use her like that. She wasn't even over her head injury. Instead, he set a steady rhythm that teased him and made it even better. He reached between them and began to lightly play with her clit. She moaned around Kent's dick, causing his brother to throw back his head and let out a hiss.

"Damn, that felt good."

"Suck his cock, Jessie. Suck it down your throat for me."

He watched as she took him all the way down. Seeing his brother's cock disappear in her mouth brought him to the edge. He struggled to hold back just a little longer. He didn't want it to be over with so soon, but her pussy began to convulse around his throbbing cock. He knew he was a goner when she began to buck as he tapped her clit with his finger. She took him over with her as he filled up her cunt with his cum.

For long seconds he couldn't move. Then he carefully pulled out and lay down beside her. She panted around Kent's cock, then redoubled her efforts at sucking his dick. He watched her throat convulse around Kent's cock over and over. He grabbed her face and began to fuck her mouth in short, quick strokes until he threw back his head and shouted as he came.

Jessie swallowed it all then licked him clean. She sighed and lay back to rest.

"I think I could take a nap now." She stretched and rolled over to wrap herself around Wyatt, laying her head on his shoulder.

It thrilled him to have her turn to him for a change. Kent grinned at him and winked. His brother was happy about it also. Kent spooned behind her and pulled her hair away from her face to kiss her neck and shoulder.

She let out a delicate little snore that had them both struggling not to laugh and wake her up.

"She's something else, isn't she?" Wyatt said.

"She's the best thing that has happened to us. It nearly killed me waiting on her to grow up," Kent confessed.

"You wouldn't have if I hadn't kept a heavy hand on you," Wyatt teased.

"It was hard because she teased us so much. She knew what she wanted even back then."

"I'm worried about winter coming up, Kent."

"Yeah, me too. This is all new to us. Brandon said he and Bolton would help us, but they have their own home to care for."

"I think it's time to go to Barter Town and trade for some chickens and another cow to build up a herd. Brandon said we're welcome to use their bull. I don't know what we would do without them, and we've only known them a week." Wyatt huffed out a breath. He didn't like depending on anyone. He'd always taken care of his little family.

"We can't take Jessie with us. We can leave her with Heather, I bet."

"Good idea. Bolton and Brandon will keep her safe."

"She's awake and listening to you," Jessie said with a yawn.

"Sorry, baby. We were just talking." Wyatt felt his face heat at being caught.

"I don't mind staying with Heather. I like her, but I don't like you saying I can't do something."

"Brandon said there are black-market men there looking to steal any female they can get their hands on. We don't want to take a chance of losing you," Wyatt explained.

"Believe me, I don't want that happening either. I've had enough excitement to last a lifetime."

"Okay. Time for you to get some sleep for real. I'm going to run and check on the animals and feed Dog." Wyatt reluctantly extracted himself from her arms and rolled out of bed.

He pulled on jeans, not bothering with thermals. He'd only be out for a few minutes.

"Be careful out there." Jessie grasped his hand and squeezed it.

"Kent, keep her warm."

"I've got it covered."

Wyatt shoved his hands into a shirt and then put on his socks and boots. He took one last look at Jessie in his brother's arms and headed downstairs to tend to the animals and make sure the house was locked up.

Nothing seemed out of place around the barn, and everything looked fine. He gave Dog food and closed the barn for the night. He walked back in the house and secured all the doors. Never again would he become complacent and take it for granted that Jessie could be snatched at any time. She was his life, and he would treat her like the precious jewel she was. Between him and his brother, they would make sure she was happy and content.

One last look and he climbed the stairs to join his family in bed.

Chapter Thirteen

Fall turned into winter with a vengeance. Snow surprised everyone, and they scrambled to get ready. Kent couldn't believe so much time had passed. They had developed a close relationship with Brandon and his family. Jessie and Heather were great friends. Wyatt had proven to be totally besotted with Jessie, and Kent enjoyed watching them together. If they could only get through this winter, they would be home free.

"What are you so deep in thought about?" Jessie asked, wrapping her arms around him from behind.

"Just thinking about this winter. Worried that we aren't prepared enough."

"Heather says we'll be just fine. Doesn't she look good pregnant?"

"She's definitely glowing." He gulped. Was Jessie trying to tell him something?

"Hey, don't look sick," she said, looking around at his face. "I'm not pregnant—yet."

"God help us if you end up pregnant anytime soon. Wyatt will have kittens himself."

Jessie giggled. "Come on. It's time for bed. I'm cold and need my men around me."

Kent didn't have to be told twice. He looked around for Wyatt but didn't see him.

"Have you seen Wyatt?"

"Hmm, not for a little while. He didn't say he was going anywhere, did he?" Jessie asked.

"Jessie, go on inside and lock the doors. I'm going to check around. He's probably somewhere working on something, but I don't want to take a chance. I don't see Dog, either."

"Kent? Please be careful."

"Get on inside, Jessie. Lock the doors, and don't open them for any reason until one of us comes back."

He watched Jessie run to the house and lock the doors. Then he headed to the barn first. Even though the door was latched on the outside, he went on in and checked to be sure he wasn't lying somewhere, hurt. Not finding him there, he closed the barn and latched it. Next was the shop. He did spend a lot of time in there. Kent walked out there and opened the door to find the room empty. Shit. His options were thinning.

Kent called out for him but received no answer, and no bark could be heard over the blowing wind that had begun to pick up. He walked out behind the garden they'd plowed under several weeks before. Surely he hadn't gone off into the woods for some reason. He couldn't leave Jessie too much longer, but he was worried about Wyatt. He wouldn't last the night in the cold if something had happened to him.

He walked out into the woods a little ways and called out. This time, he heard the answering bark of Dog. He called out again, and Wyatt and Dog appeared. Wyatt had a gun with him.

"Where in the hell have you been? I've been looking everywhere for you, and Jessie is scared to death something has happened to you."

"Sorry, I went in farther than I had planned. Saw a wolf and went after it, but I lost it."

"Don't need one this close to the house, that's for sure. I don't want the same thing to happen to Jessie that happened to Heather." Kent shuddered at the thought.

"What are we going to do?" Wyatt asked.

"Well, Jessie can't go out by herself at all until we hunt him down, that's for sure."

"I'm going to talk to Brandon and Bolton tomorrow about it. It's close enough to their neck of the woods as well." Wyatt nodded toward the house. "Better get home before Jessie decides to come looking for us. I'd hate to have to spank her ass."

"Hmm, I don't know. She might like it," Kent said with a chuckle.

"What do you think about anal sex?" Wyatt asked Kent.

"Hell, man. I want in her ass so bad, I could die, but I don't want to hurt her."

"If we're careful, it shouldn't really hurt. You know that. We've done it often enough in the past."

"Yea, but this is Jessie," Kent reminded him.

"I know." Wyatt sighed. "I can't help but want to give her the best ride of her life."

"We'll see how she reacts to being prepared. If she's not into it, I'm not pushing her, Wyatt."

"Hell, no. I wouldn't do that for anything."

"Come on. She's probably frantic by now."

* * * *

Jessie curled around Kent, waiting on Wyatt to come to bed after his shower. He always went downstairs and checked all the locks for a second time. She thought it was overprotective of him but didn't say anything. She liked feeling safe.

He came running up the stairs and all but jumped in the bed. Kent and Jessie squeezed up to keep him from landing on them. They all died laughing.

"What's gotten into you tonight?" Jessie asked, climbing on top of him.

"Just glad it's snuggle time." He wiggled his eyebrows. "How about you ride me, cowgirl?"

"Yippie aye ay." She started to climb on his hardened dick, but Kent stopped her.

"No you don't. Not yet. I want to prep that pussy first. You just lie down on Wyatt."

"I'm all wet and ready now, Kent."

"Humor me, baby."

Jessie stuck her tongue out at him but complied. She licked and nibbled on Wyatt's chest and nipples until she had him squirming. Then she was the one squirming as Kent began playing with her pussy. He tickled her clit with his finger, then plunged two of them inside her. She moaned and laid her head down on Wyatt's chest, just trying to breathe around the pleasure. He fucked her cunt with his fingers, then stroked her hot spot until she was about ready to come.

Then, she felt him circle her back hole. She stilled as he gathered her juices and spread them around her ass. He slowly pushed his thumb inward.

"Push out for me, baby. Let me in."

Jessie wanted this. She wanted both of her men filling her and hadn't known how to bring it up. They were doing it for her. She pushed out and his thumb popped in past the ring of resistance. He began pushing it in and out. Then he pulled it free, and she felt a cold gel squeezed in her ass. She shivered.

Kent pushed a finger inside of her ass. Soon he was pushing in and pulling out over and over. Then he added a second one. It burned, but she could handle a little burn. He shoved them in and out, spreading them to prepare her for his thick cock. When he added a third finger, she thought she would cry out with the tremendous burn, but it gave way to something far better. She felt nerve endings coming alive. She couldn't help it. She began to push back against him.

"Jessie, climb on top of Wyatt now, baby. Slide his cock inside of you."

Jessie carefully moved to position Wyatt's massive dick at her slit and then slowly lowered herself until she was sitting all the way on him. Kent pushed her down to lie on Wyatt's chest. Wyatt wrapped his arms around her back and whispered how proud he was of her and how good it was going to feel to have both of them filling her.

Kent pushed in the three fingers over and over. She could feel them against the thin membrane separating his fingers from Wyatt's cock. The sensations were awesome. She couldn't handle much more. She begged Kent to fill her.

Kent pulled his fingers out, and she felt the head of his cock at her back door. He began to push in against her ass. She pushed out, trying to accommodate his massive size. It burned so badly. Then he popped through and stilled to let her get used to him. She breathed out and began moving back against him. She needed him to move. He took her hint and pulled almost all the way out, then plunged back in.

She could feel her men sliding back and forth inside of her. Never had she felt so full. Finally, she felt truly connected to them. They were whole now. When Wyatt pulled out, Kent pushed in, and then Wyatt pushed in while Kent pulled out. They suspended her between them, doing all the work. She felt nerve endings all over come alive. Wyatt rasped over that hot spot again and again.

She knew she was going to come and fought it. It was too much. She would splinter into a million tiny pieces if she came.

"Oh, God. I'm going to die. It feels too good."

"Fuck, you're tight. I can't hold on much longer, Wyatt."

"Neither can I. Come for us, Jessie. Come on, baby," Wyatt said in a strained voice.

"I can't. It's too much."

Wyatt reached between them and pinched her clit. She soared higher than she'd ever been before. She felt her men come inside of her, filling her with their hot cum. It was the last straw. Everything went black.

* * * *

"She's going to be so mad that she passed out like that," Kent said.

"Hell, she scared me to death when she suddenly went limp and wouldn't answer me."

"Man, that was the most intense feeling I've ever experienced."

"Tell me about it. I thought I was going to come until I turned inside out," Wyatt admitted.

"Hey, she's coming 'round."

"What happened to me?" Jessie whispered.

"You passed out. If you're going to do that every time we both come in you, we can't do it anymore," Kent teased her.

"Like hell. That was amazing. I'll get used to it."

"I hope you don't," Wyatt fussed. "I want it to amaze you every time."

"I don't think you have to worry about that." She squeezed Wyatt's hand then Kent's.

"We're finally a family, the three of us and Dog."

THE END

WWW.MARLAMONROE.COM

ABOUT THE AUTHOR

Marla Monroe lives in the southern part of the United States. She writes sexy romance from the heart and often puts a twist of suspense in her books. She is a nurse and works in a busy hospital, but finds plenty of time to follow her two passions, reading and writing. You can find her in a book store or a library at any given time when she's not at work or writing. Marla would love for you to visit her at her blog at themarlamonroe.blogspot.com and leave a comment.

Also by Marla Monroe

Ménage Everlasting: Men of the Border Lands 1: *Belonging to Them*
Ménage Everlasting: Men of the Border Lands 3:
Their Border Lands Temptress

For all other titles, please visit
www.bookstrand.com/marla-monroe

Siren Publishing, Inc.
www.SirenPublishing.com

CPSIA information can be obtained at www.ICGtesting.com
Printed in the USA
BVOW03s1710220414

351380BV00012B/318/P